PROTECT HER

PROTECT HER

Come for Me, Prequel Novelette

KELLY FINLEY

© 2021 Kelly Finley Publishing, LLC
Visit the author's website at kellyfinley.com
ISBN: 978-1-7374516-3-1 (eBook)
978-1-7374516-2-4 (paperback
All rights reserved.

No part of this publication may be reproduced, distributed, or transmitted in any form or by any means, stored in or introduced into a retrieval system, or transmitted, in any form including photocopying, recording, or other electronic or mechanical methods, without the prior written permission of the above author of this book.

This is a work of fiction. Names, characters, places, brands, media, and incidents are either the product of the author's imagination or have been used fictitiously. Any resemblance to actual persons, living or dead, events, or locales is entirely coincidental.

The author acknowledges the trademarked status and trademark owners of various products referenced in this work of fiction, which have been used without permission. The publication/use of these trademarks is not authorized, associated with, or sponsored by the trademark owners.

Proofreading by Kat Wyeth, Kat's Literary Services

Cover & Interior Design by Caroline Johnson

PROTECT HER PLAYLIST

"Souls" by Bones UK
"Our Time" by Lily Allen
"Mother's Daughter" (R3HAB Remix) by Miley Cyrus
"La Noche De Anoche" by Bad Bunny x ROSALÍA
"Bastards" by Kesha
"Ditch" by Empara Mi
"Let Me Know Now" by Silver Swans
"Surrender to Love" by Ottmar Liebert
"Gold" by MILCK
"Woman" (feat. The Dap-Kings Horns) by Kesha

<u>Listen to the Protect Her playlist on Spotify</u>

This book is dedicated to the friends who bring smiles to my days and trouble to my nights. Your proud and fearless support fuels my soul and so many pages. You know who you are (cuz' you're laughing and feeling not guilty right now). I love you all!

In humble gratitude and with great respect, ten percent of all proceeds gratefully earned from this book series will be donated to the non-profit organization <u>AMVETS-Sheroes on the Move</u>.

ONE

)

Suspicion was her default setting despite the glamorous, sex-drenched scene. No temptation could drop her guard. No threat could deter her. If a man aimed her way, she'd aim right back. Like her stare now, hidden behind her gold Aviators... it was clocking his every subtle move.

Charlie Ravenel mapped the man's gaze straight to Juliette, down to the drink swirling in his hand, back up again to Juliette's ass perched on a white lounger in the golden Ibiza Island sunlight. She read his posture, his expression. How a soft side-grin wouldn't leave his handsome face. How his brown eyes widened, intrigued by the celebrity spectacle in front of him. That his elbows were propped on his tan knees, the tendons in his feet poised to move. The tension glistening across his sculpted shoulders urged the same. She read it all like a suspense novel—how he intended to rise though he sat on the edge of his chair, wavering.

"Someone's watchin' you." Charlie moved her bare feet

from resting on her lounger down onto the teak-wood pool deck, muscles ready to pounce, her gaze still judging him.

Innocent fingertips strummed over his glass of sangria. A guilty tip of his tongue licked his lips before teeth took his bottom lip prisoner in a pensive, sexy bite. The hot man's body was screaming with desire to approach his target, but his eyebrows pinched, confidence detained.

Juliette's reply was muffled by her plush, white towel. "Charlie, my love, the man is smitten with you. You look like a sexy, blonde cowgirl ready to ride the next hunk of man flesh off into the sunset."

Yeah, right. That's horseshit.

Juliette wasn't even looking at him. Topless and relaxing on her belly, she laid, ass beckoning in a red bikini bottom smaller than her megawatt smile.

Not Charlie. She was doing her job, protecting Juliette. From under her straw cowgirl hat, she reclined back on her chair, her scrutiny concealed by mirrored shades. The sure feeling of being targeted by a man tingled across her skin. *That* and a warm breeze caressing her legs barely revealed by her white, Kimono cover-up. Compulsion to hide her body never dulled. With a quick tug, she checked its knot, securing it around her waist in case she had to intercept.

"If he's so smitten with me, then tell that to his eyes that won't stop staring at you like dessert." Charlie's suspicion started to dull into amusement at the stand-off with the admirer. "He's licking up the view of your ass cheeks like a damn, vanilla ice cream cone. I give him ten minutes before he comes over for a bite."

"I wish. No one ever approaches me anymore."

Juliette propped up on her elbows, directing her gaze and famous, perfect tits to the cliff overlooking the azure Mediterranean Sea. "Bloody ironic it is. Three years ago, I was pushing blokes off me, barely scraping by, career stalled so I had to pull pints at a dodgy London bar. And now I have thirty million followers, a number one show, and you're the only one who still talks to me like I'm a real person. And you're my bloody bodyguard."

"I'm your bloody bodyguard who you happily seduced into being your best friend too, thank you very much. A friend you swore to, that while we're on vacation for hiatus, you were getting laid in Ibiza." Her chin gestured to the arousing opportunity across the hotel's turquoise pool. "There's your chance, chica."

"*No*, I swore we were *both* getting laid this week." The red Cartier sunglasses masking Juliette's jade eyes turned her way. "Come on, Charlie. Enjoy the week with me. You deserve it too. Let's both get properly fucked before we go back to ten more weeks of filming. We're on holiday in sexy Ibiza. We're supposed to be dancing, drinking and fucking like mad. Yet, here I lie, the only one topless, arse-out and drinking."

"Oh, don't you worry 'bout me. My imagination is ass-out and gettin' laid, but my clothes stay on. You know why. We may be on vacation, but I relax like a dog with a bone."

Charlie sipped her iced coffee. Her pupils were still lingering over the man with the smooth, carved chest. Still counting his eight-pack abs, ones she wanted to soap up and wash her white, lace thongs on. Still wandering her gaze down to his pink swim trunks, curious what pleasure they concealed. They made her grin. Any man confident enough to wear pastel pink and make it look *that* sexy has gotta be a good fuck.

"But I promise to stand down if Captain Penis in Pink Passion Pants comes over here for a piece of you," she said.

That made Juliette laugh and glance back over her shoulder at the sight Charlie had been monitoring for the past hour. And it made Juliette smile. And it made her shake her cheeky ass in the sunlight at him. And *that* made him look down at his drink, grinning at her invitation.

"I think he's a bit shy," Charlie said. "That makes him even hotter."

"I think I have a Non-Disclosure Agreement in my beach bag ready for him to sign before he gives me a good rogering."

Charlie chuckled at the protocol. The NDAs Juliette and so many famous people had to use to protect their privacy, secrets and careers were par for the celebrity course. Normal people can meet someone at a bar and maybe get an innocent, steamy fuck that night. Perhaps it becomes a relationship. Perhaps it's only a night. But Juliette's life ceased being normal two years before. She debuted as the star of *Fated*, a fantasy television series that captivated the globe's attention with its epic saga. And with its popularity and Juliette's staggering beauty, she hadn't lived a normal moment since.

"I've got you covered if you wanna give him a ride." Charlie tipped her hat to him. "It would give me a chance to give him a good pat down for hidden weapons." He grinned back at the pair of women across the sparkling pool, obviously talking about him. "Besides, you might as well put your luxury, two-bedroom suite by the sea to use."

"It's a two-bedroom suite for a reason, my love." Juliette flipped over, flipping open her invitation to him even more. "You have your own empty bed that could use some company tonight too."

"I can't. I've got a job to do. I'm covering you and your pussy on the prowl."

This was too fun, a true vacation for Charlie.

Kicking back by a pool, winding up her friend, she watched with delight from the sidelines of Juliette's celebrity life. A life Charlie never wanted but encouraged Juliette to live to its max. Covering Juliette with this morsel of a man would be an easy, risk-free night. A true break from guarding her against real threats when they were back in London or Belfast filming.

"Don't make me prowl alone, bitch," Juliette said while the scent of coconut drifted through the air. She was spraying more sunscreen body oil over her naked breasts. "It's not fun if I'm the only one having it. I hate it when I see you alone, hiding in the shadows, watching me at parties or clubs. I stand there, wishing you could join me, wanting you to be happy too."

The slick sight of Juliette's now-glazed tits made the man adjust his bathing suit. The gesture forced Charlie's cheeks high in a smile, thoroughly entertained by this tease. "I'm as happy as I can be with you, chica. Don't worry 'bout me. Compared to the last five years of my life, this is a constant party."

Juliette reached her small, shiny hand out for hers.

Charlie took it. The two friends didn't need to say it. Both knew what each had survived, what hell had brought each to this heavenly moment. "Then let's make this next year glorious," Juliette said. "If that hot bloke comes over, I'll share him with you."

The notion made Charlie laugh. "I appreciate your generosity, but Captain Pink Penis over there is all yours."

"It better not be pink!" Juliette rolled back with laughter. "It better be a tan, long, thick knob with staying power, enough for us both to enjoy."

"The poor guy. You're making him sound like a mechanical bull."

"Bloody right! A hard, twenty-minute ride for us both." Juliette lowered her sunglasses, a mischievous smile curved across her face. "Yee-haw, bitch. You already have the hat on."

Charlie's abs started to hurt with the laughter tensing across them, a pain she relished. "I love you… but hell no."

"Rob can cover us both." The pitch in Juliette's voice was joking while she nodded over to the massive man asleep on the other side of her. "He's napping now to work tonight. Come on, Charlie, let your gorgeous hair down and have some fun with me."

"Our little threesome is getting too close and comfortable." Charlie shook her head, half amused and half concerned, leaning forward to check Rob's position.

His tree trunk legs were stacked over big, booted feet on the pool deck, ready to jump up and defend, but his eyelids laid soft with slumber. Nope, Charlie was on-deck now protecting Juliette. "We're supposed to be your security, not your best friends."

"Too late. I fancy you as both. With everything we've been through this year. With every time you've saved me. Bloody hell, the times we've saved each other. You're forever in my heart and life, bitch."

Charlie grinned over at Juliette. "Backatcha, bitch. Forever."

She didn't see the tawny-tressed, A-list actress. The one with striking dark eyebrows over green eyes and a signature smile that took over her entire petite face and the world's heart.

No, Charlie saw a woman in danger. A woman she was hired to protect from sick stalkers and crazed fans threatening Juliette's every move. She saw a woman who lived in a prison of celebrity and suffered it all with gratitude, kindness and humor.

And now, after a year together, she saw a woman who had become her dearest friend, safety protocol be damned. You're not supposed to get close to your mark, the one you are hired to protect. It can cloud your judgement, distracting you, relaxing you into making a lethal mistake. Not for Charlie. All her love for Juliette did was make her even more fiercely protective over her.

Because Juliette knew. Knew after a horrific day on set months back that brought Charlie to her knees. *That* was when Charlie stopped being only her bodyguard. *That* was when Juliette found out Charlie's darkest secret, saw her hidden scars, helped her wipe away grieving tears, heard her story, and only hugged her tighter for it.

After *that*, Charlie would do more than protect Juliette.

She'd take another bullet for her.

"Heads up, horny girl," Charlie muttered from the side of her mouth. The seductive man was finally rising, mustering his courage to engage their imposing threesome. "Told you. Ten minutes and he's headin' this way. Get out some lube, an NDA, and prepare to be rogered alright."

Yep. Charlie's suspicion was always fact.

TWO

)

A forkful of saffron risotto halted in front of Charlie's lips. "I like him but not his friends," she said. "Not that blond one. He's got all kinds of wrong dripping off him."

She was supposed to be enjoying her dinner, letting Juliette do the same with the sexy new friend she had made that day. But Charlie's track record of doing what she was supposed to was shot all to hell.

Santiago was the name of the admirer by the pool.

His approach earlier that afternoon had been a delight for Charlie to witness. Loving that she was right. Loving that Juliette may get her wish. Pushing her red sunglasses atop her head before extending her gold, French manicured tips for a greeting; Juliette's welcoming smile had offered Santiago a fighting chance. And he took it. Gently kissing her hand, making a good impression, he had respectfully introduced himself, eyes meeting Juliette's and not her bare tits.

Attraction stole Juliette and approval hit Charlie.

But tonight, as Juliette sat with Santiago and his two friends joining them for dinner on the patio of the boutique hotel's restaurant, Charlie enjoyed the situation like a root-canal… without Novocain. The tines of the fork crossed over her lips. She almost bit the metal.

Something felt off.

"She's a grown woman and we got her covered. Let her have fun," Rob said before loading his fork up with a bite of blue lobster and couscous, while the delicious risotto danced across Charlie's palate. "You should have your fun too. While you're so busy scoping Juliette and her dinner guests, that man at four o'clock won't stop scoping you out either."

Charlie glanced over her right shoulder, catching what Rob surveilled.

Holy shit. She had to admit to herself. *Yes, Charlie Girl. That succulent man is a drink in the desert.*

Long black waves. Confident, mature eyes. White, linen shirt unbuttoned, revealing a tan oasis. All this while his lush, wise smile lingered over her with a tempting gaze.

"Why is everyone so hell bent on getting me laid?" Charlie turned back, reaching for a sip of sparkling water instead, putting her focus back to Juliette's table.

"Because if Juliette is our alluring celebrity mark to protect, then you're her enticing protection officer who can't hide her beauty under any hat *or* on any set." Rob's grin back at her was full of warmth and respect but his eyes twinkled, playfully.

Damn, she loved him. Working with Rob didn't feel like effort. It felt like home.

Rob's chin nodded toward the man. The one whose admiration warmed the skin over Charlie's shoulder. "You can have him or anyone you want. How long you gonna wait 'til you get you some again?"

Eyes down to her plate, down to so much pain, a sudden wave washed over her. A wave of grief Rob knew about and protected too. "I'm not ready yet."

"I get that. But it's been over two years." A sip of his Café Bombón offered a needed pause before he said, "Just promise me *yet* doesn't become *never*."

"We'll see." She leaned back in her chair, letting the heartache wash through. Her gaze back to Juliette helped. Not giving a shit about her own sex life, Charlie was too focused on protecting the one Juliette tried to have.

Santiago sat comfortably by Juliette's side, his smile and eyes wouldn't leave her brilliant profile. He posed no threat to Juliette. Charlie was sure.

But that blond guy and his date? Something twitched across Charlie's nerves. Instinct told her with certainty— *that man is a risk.*

And the young woman with him? She seemed nervous.

Maybe it was because she was sitting across from Juliette Jones— the woman whose face was plastered across every magazine cover and screen. It made almost everyone either pathetically bend over backwards for Juliette or keep a gawking distance from her. Either way, few treated Juliette like the big-hearted woman with a bawdy sense of humor who never took herself seriously that she was.

That was the Juliette, the friend, that Charlie loved, but not the one she protected.

Charlie and Rob worked for HGR Security. They were brought onto the set of *Fated* the year before to protect her. Once Juliette debuted as one of the stars of the massive hit show, she could no longer walk a London sidewalk without risk hounding her. Fanatics hungered for Juliette like she was their last meal. Paparazzi tried to claim her every moment, her privacy, and her sanity. Threats reached, grabbing like they were entitled to every piece of Juliette's beautiful body too.

It was a lecherous reality Charlie shared with her. It's why she and Juliette grew so close, so fast.

Two years before, serving in Afghanistan, Charlie had been hunted too.

Hell, Charlie was pursued her whole life. Bullied. Teased because she never fit into her South Carolina Lowcountry culture. She was no sweet, Southern belle. She was a tanned tomboy with long, blonde locks bleached to almost white from days on the water around her small island home.

If it wasn't mean words hitting Charlie, it was groping hands in the halls of high school. Or leering eyes in the college classroom. Or threats hissed low at Boot Camp. Later, it was actual weapons aimed at her.

She had survived them all so far.

And now, nothing would keep her from making sure Juliette survived the same.

Santiago started nuzzling into Juliette's neck, whispering in her ear. The grin on Juliette's face told Charlie she consented. So, Charlie's posture stilled, watching while her thighs tensed ready to leap, while her left fist clenched, prepared to neutralize any threat to her friend.

Rob filled the heavy silence in the air with their favorite topic of conversation, sex—or in Charlie's case—the lack thereof.

"I don't know how you do it. How you've gone so long without a fuck and some good D." He tried humoring her out of the bad memories.

"Oh, I can go without the D. All I need is a vibrating double A." Charlie taunted back.

"You can play with all the toys you want, it's not the same. If I were a woman and looked like you, my playground would be full of the real thing. Every fucking night I'd sit and spin."

That made her laugh. Rob always pushed aside her fuck-off vibe, finding her true, warm heart behind the curtain.

It's like he saw it the minute they met, saw all they had in common. The day they were both recruited by HGR, he reached out his massive hand, greeting his colleague with respect and soon, both found deep friendship and loyalty too.

"Sounds like you need a new place to play." She loaded up her fork again. This conversation was making her hungry. "You know, it'd be easy for you to find another playmate. With that iron physique, you're a damn Disney Park of sucks and fucks."

That tossed his chin back, deep loud laughter rolling over his boulders for pecs. "Oh, mi prima. I love you too much to let you keep hiding, all horny and alone. We *both* need to come out and play."

"I'm just fine alone, hiding and horny." Amusement

wafted through the air between them, but she meant it.

Hidden beneath the naughty banter, there was nothing but fear for Charlie. Terror that she had better hide either on her secluded, island home or in the shadows of dark stage building. It haunted her. That her secret from years before wasn't dead. That it would come back for her. The only thing that kept her sane was that she hoped she was wrong. That it was just her diagnosed paranoia, not a maddening prophecy.

Nope. Don't bullshit yourself, Charlie Girl. It's not your PTSD. It's fate. You used up your luck last time. Use your head now. The best tactic? Never be lured out to play.

"No go, Captain." Rob wouldn't relent. "I'm not letting you hide all alone. After this season wraps, you're taking that trip with me. Home to visit my abuela in Santo Domingo. Best empanadas you've ever had."

That offer she couldn't refuse. Going back to her home hurt too much. All that greeted her there was ghosts and grief. And guilt. Yes, she loved her Lowcountry home and close friends there, but her broken heart couldn't bear the full weight of a normal life yet. Whatever the hell that was anymore, she didn't know. So, following Juliette or Rob around the globe, running from it all? That sounded like a sure plan for now.

"I'm game," she said. "Just as long as I get to sit back and watch you play your games too. Watch you unleash all that hotness upon the Caribbean shores. It'll be fucking Hurricane Rob coming. Batten down your pants and hatches, folks."

"Deal." He raised his glass to seal it. "Speaking of, we

have a visitor."

Rob's handsome golden face flashed a bright white grin, signaling to whomever approached—we're not a threat, and yes, you're very welcome to join us.

"Excuse me." A husky Spanish accent strummed like a flamenco guitar over Charlie's earlobe. "I'm dining alone this evening but wondered if I may join your friendly table for dessert."

Flax-colored linen pants entered Charlie's peripheral vision. An elegant, manicured masculine hand gestured to the back of the empty chair beside her. She glanced up to find rich brown eyes rimmed by thick lashes under dark eyebrows as full of curiosity as his rose lips were full of promise.

Damnation, Charlie Girl. This proximity of this man would melt anyone's butter.

But not hers. Her body sat cool and unaffected.

"Please, join us." Rob took over the pleasantries, gesturing for the polite guest to take a seat.

"This is my fifth time here," their new guest shared, pulling out the chair next to hers. "And I must insist, their rosemary ice cream deserves to be enjoyed in good company." Lowering himself beside Charlie, reaching his hand out to shake Rob's, he said, "Gabriel Duran."

"Rob Vasquez." He returned his handshake, gesturing next toward Charlie's soft smile and numb body. "And this is my colleague, Charlie Ravenel."

Gabriel's palm called out for hers. "Pleasure to meet you, Mrs. Ravenel."

Her skin met his demand, met warm suede in his touch.

"Nice to meet you too, Mr. Duran." All she indulged was the polite ritual, noting how his greeting also sought intel on her marital status. "And thank you, but I'm not a Mrs. I'm a Ms. I'm a widow." There. That kept men at an intimidated distance. She smiled then put her eyes back to Juliette.

"I see we also have a famous dinner guest here tonight." Gabriel smoothed past the awkward, Charlie tried serving up. Instead, following her gaze, he gestured toward Juliette's table. "Are you fans of her show? I think the entire world, like myself, is captivated by it."

"We work for Ms. Jones and the studio producing the show," Rob informed him.

Gabriel's eyebrows shot up. "Oh. You're her bodyguards?" He gestured toward Charlie's feet barely tucked under the table. "That explains why you're wearing jeans and tactical boots and not a lovely dress with sandals by the ocean."

That impressed Charlie.

The man was observant. That made him smart.

But he was observing her. That made him a risk.

"Yes, we're her security." Rob reached out to sip his café, not taking his eyes off their new dinner guest while Charlie's remained on their mark. Remained on that blond guy across from Juliette.

The smile on that blond creep's face betrayed a smirk in his eyes. The logic behind them was a calculating comb over Juliette's tempting form in a white sundress.

Charlie's teeth sank into the truth, ripping at the flesh and fact like a lioness killing her prey. *He's a threat. Not just to Juliette. To all women.* She fucking knew it, always trusting her instinct, betting on it like the sunrise every morning.

What did instinct tell her right then?

This guy—Gabriel, to Charlie's right—he's a risk, but not a harmful one. No, he was tempting her. Wanting her. But not now. And sorry Rob, maybe *never*.

Santiago? Sitting beside Juliette? He's sex served on a silver platter. Surely, he would be a delicious fuck for Juliette that night. No threat unless he fell in love with Juliette. Almost all did who came within feet of her captivating smile.

The young woman at Juliette's table? She was rubber bands wrapped up in a ball, wound tight and about to snap. With what, Charlie wondered. The woman wouldn't stop glancing nervously over at Charlie, then darting her eyes away.

Concern for the strange young woman festered through Charlie's bones.

Her stare met the young woman's next glance. *Yep, that's it. You know the look in a woman's eye, Charlie Girl… she's afraid.* But her bare toes kept playing footsie up the leg of her suspicious dinner date. Not like she was afraid of him. Then what?

Him though? The blond? His name was Martin.

Charlie had overheard him introduce himself to Juliette when they joined her for dinner. The attention he put on Juliette flared Charlie's nostrils. The young woman shook Juliette's hand like a wet rag, barely uttering that her name was Lindy. Then Martin offered an introductory kiss to Juliette's cheek, one that lasted too long by Charlie's measure.

That Martin guy smelled as right as fish lying in the July sun for five days. Despite the alluring distraction sitting beside Charlie, her focus remained on her suspicion—Martin and Lindy.

In her periphery, Gabriel crossed his legs like a gentleman with money and manners. "I work in the energy industry, wind power mainly. Not very exciting. So, I must confess that I'm intrigued. How does one become a bodyguard?" His regard returned to Charlie. "From the boots up, you certainly don't look like one."

Charlie caught it on her left. How Rob glanced at her, eyes prodding for her to reply, to engage their sexy dinner guest. Charlie didn't budge. Silence sat in her mouth.

Rob jumped in with his warm smile and gravel voice. "That's what makes us a good pair. Threats see me coming from a mile away while she's a stealth bomber, sneaking in low and undetected."

The compliment made Gabriel rake his fingers through his long strands, pausing with a grin Charlie's way. "You're former military?"

"I am," Rob said.

Shit, Rob wasn't discouraging this. It was like he was trying to sell her to Gabriel like a brand-new red Ferrari, one with an engine that wouldn't turn. Rob's boot nudged hers under the table. "And she's a stone you can't break. One with perfect aim."

"Oh, so you've got good aim too, Ms. Ravenel?" Gabriel asked.

She noticed. Noticed how Gabriel wasn't dissuaded by her stoic response, keeping pace with the intel he gathered, seeking even more. He called her with respect by her unmarried designation now. Guess her being a widow didn't intimidate him. That raised Charlie's eyebrow, impressed.

But she wouldn't bite. She had no appetite for this.

The pleasure and pain waiting at the end of this road was too familiar, too fresh for her. She needed more time. More time to build her walls higher so that no one could climb them.

"Yes, I do have good aim."

Still, she answered him. Her guard wasn't Gabriel's fault. His attempt was valiant. Charming too. Reaching for another sip of water, she offered him a genuine smile, one that softened her face, crinkling the long scar down her right cheek. "But I won't work with guns anymore. I've had enough of them."

"So, you *are* former military?"

His lush Spanish accent was thick with esteem. And desire. It made any question from his mouth sound like an invitation to bed. Hell, years ago… he could have asked her opinion on tax policy and seduced her into letting him audit her entire body with more than words all night long.

But that was a lifetime ago. A lifetime Charlie had almost lost. And would never risk again. Not for a man. Even a sexy one that seemed so impressed, so interested in her.

Her eyes turned away from his unanswered question, back to her mark. Juliette put her napkin on her plate before casually tenting her fingertips in front of her cleavage.

That was the signal. The one they had planned.

"Please excuse me, gentlemen." Charlie stood, addressing her colleague and their beguiling dinner guest with, "Duty calls." Dedication to the job always defeated her desire.

THREE

)

"Are you sure you want to do this?" Charlie wasn't shaming her friend's curiosity and kink. She was only concerned for her safety.

"Yes. I've never done anything like this. I never do anything crazy or for myself." Juliette squirted a line of minty paste over the bristles of her toothbrush. "But just this once, I'm going to. With no apologies. No regrets."

It was true. Juliette was the most unselfish person Charlie had ever met.

Juliette had cared for her mother before she died of cancer. She cared now for her adult brother who needed a full-time ward. She cared for the cast and crew depending upon the show Juliette starred in, for paychecks to feed their family. Any extra hours in her life she donated to charity causes or friends who needed her. Juliette worked hard every day, worrying about everyone, laden with the responsibility of it all. And the only indulgence Charlie had ever witnessed her enjoy was a weekly mani/pedi.

Except now.

Juliette's little red Corvette was speeding toward fun, gunning from zero to Mach four with one racy plan. And she deserved it.

"Besides." Suds in Juliette's mouth frothed over her pink lips. "Male celebrities. Rockstars. Royalty. All kinds of rich arseholes do it all time. Why can't I? They get away with a lifetime of crazy sex and I want just one night. I haven't had a good shag in months. And now I can have two, maybe three."

She spat in the sink of her suite's spa bathroom while Charlie leaned against its door, hearing the guests outside in the living area mixing their drinks while Rob guarded outside.

Juliette rinsed her mouth before she gushed the words, "I've only kissed one woman so far. And the one tonight, Lindy, she's so beautiful, so alluring. And those men are so fit. They've all signed NDAs, I have a box of condoms and give a mountain of consent for whatever is next."

Juliette's eyes danced with lurid anticipation. It took Charlie a minute to process, to prepare. Not judging her friend's desire, only judging her exposure.

"I'm not leaving you alone and unguarded with three strangers. It's too much risk. They could overpower you and I wouldn't be able to hear you and know if you're being harmed."

"All right, then. You keep their phones secured and you cover me inside the suite. Rob sits outside the door."

Juliette unzipped her sundress, letting it drop to the floor, standing before her in a lacy, lavender bra and panty set. "I'm doing this, Charlie. Santiago suggested it and I think I've lost my fucking mind, but I don't care. My randy cunt is ready. Just once I'm doing something X-rated and crazy—a true holiday-in-Ibiza romp."

"Look, bitch. You don't owe me an explanation. You go for it, and I'll get your back. But I'm just saying… I don't like that Martin guy."

"He is blond and brooding, isn't he? It makes him so fucking hot."

"No. It makes him a fucking risk. I trust hot men like skating on thin ice. Beauty breeds them with entitlement. And entitled men are dangerous men. And I don't trust that woman either. She's beautiful but nervous… and mousy women make my ass twitch. Something is going on with her."

"Charlie, I love you for always watching out for me, but relax. What's the worst they can do if you're nearby? You'll have their phones. There'll be no pictures, no harm tonight. Not with you and Rob protecting me and not with an iron-clad agreement keeping my fun little secret."

Charlie's pulse started racing. The foursome her mark and friend was preparing to have made Charlie nervous. The sex didn't worry her. The uncertainty did.

It was one thing guarding Juliette on set. Quietly standing in the shadows of a stage building or on a location behind Juliette's cast chair—those were settings Charlie controlled. Even in a swanky club or at an A-list party, Charlie was prepared, knew all exit routes and timelines in advance.

She had already taken down multiple threats to Juliette.

Once at a coffee shop in Knightsbridge, a fan tried to corner Juliette in the restroom, demanding she date him, marry him, fuck him, be his until death. That guy was deranged. And Charlie had him stumbling away from the bathroom doorway, pissing his pants in pain after she delivered a deft eye gouge.

And the stalker who grabbed Juliette's breast outside a London bar? Charlie had dropped him to his knees with a throat punch before squatting down beside him, twisting his balls, whispering a warning in his ear. Too easy.

Tonight?

This was different, new territory for them both.

Yes, Juliette had had a few dates leading to a couple of overnight, vetted guests that past year. But that was planned. This was provocative. Of what? Charlie feared provoking touches gone too far, provoking harm, not pleasure. It had Charlie running a lightning-fast assessment of how this could play out all while keeping Juliette safe and secure.

"All doors stay open. You stay in my line of sight." Charlie planned her tactics. "If one of them shuts or locks anything closed, I swear I will break that shit down and choke them all out, orgasms be damned. Deal?"

"Deal." Juliette's eyebrows lifted while she bit her lip. Excited. Nervous. Horny. "I can't believe I'm doing this."

"You aren't doing anything you don't want to. Just be loud and shout my name if anything goes too far. If it's not what you want, I'll stop it."

"Well… there's no stopping me now." Juliette gave her a quick peck on the cheek, reaching for the bathroom doorknob. "One of us needs to get properly fucked. I guess it has to be me."

"Thanks for taking one—wait, no—I mean *three* for the team." Charlie started laughing. Happy for Juliette's joy and sex, two things absent from her own life.

But that didn't stop the two men from trying her. While Juliette stripped down and stepped naked into the large outdoor Jacuzzi on the suite's balcony under the night sky, Santiago kept looking over at Charlie.

She tried hiding in the shadows, sitting on the low, white sofa by the suite door while Rob guarded outside of it. The wall of sliding glass doors fifteen feet away from her were all opened to the balcony with a glass railing to the ocean beyond and the stars above.

Nothing blocked her path to Juliette except for Santiago's form standing there. It was an invitation embossed with sex at the threshold between where Charlie sat, and the others stripped outside. His handsome head canted to the side, his hard muscles and cock taunting her. "Want to join us?" he asked.

For a man who seemed so shy that afternoon, he sure was bold with intent that night.

"I'm fine," Charlie said, appreciating the lewd sight mere feet in front of her.

That's all it was to her—a sight. She had been surrounded by men her whole life. Covered in blood. Covered with nothing. They never intimidated her. Not on the job. All that stood before her were vulnerable points of masculine flesh she could punch, kick, knee, gouge or choke to protect Juliette.

Martin stood behind Santiago, his hand cupping his girlfriend's naked ass while his eyes roamed over Charlie too. "Yes, you are fine." His chin lowered. "Real fucking fine."

"Leave her be." Juliette called out from the Jacuzzi. "She's here for me, not you lot."

"Lucky for you," Martin said to Juliette. "You get to use her for protection *and* to fuck."

"Hey, asshole." Charlie had heard enough from him… and he had only just spoken to her. "Keep talking about me like I'm a piece of ass and this will be your most unlucky night ever."

Her threat made Santiago laugh while he stepped over the ledge of the Jacuzzi, joining Juliette with a long row of condoms gripped in his hand. Lindy, the nude ball of nerves, followed behind Santiago, glancing intimidated over at Charlie.

But Martin remained erect and aimed toward her.

"Trust me." Juliette called out to him. "You don't want to take her on. Not for a fuck or a fight. You won't win."

Ah, her dear friend knew her too well.

Charlie sat stoic, eyes firing at Martin until their glare turned him away. Turned him back toward the Jacuzzi to start the night full of fucking fun for Juliette.

FOUR

Cygnus. Lyra. Hercules.

Charlie occupied herself naming the constellations in the summer sky. A skill her mother had taught her many years before. She missed her. Now, the sky was her only familiar company while nude bodies swam, laughed, kissed, and then started licking and sucking everything they desired.

The sight and sound of Juliette's pleasure made her happy. And a little horny. And a little wet. A tingle between her thighs started, one she would later reliably satisfy on her own. Moans of lust filled the night air, firing her memory with the last time Charlie had sex.

No, *that* time was making love. Love she hadn't felt in over two years.

The night was a passionate, desperate moment stolen away for a few hours from war. Umber eyes cherishing hers, tears both shed for never enough time shared. Kisses full of hurried worship, tongues wanting to cling to more than flesh. His skillful hand sliding slick over her begging need, fingers plunging inside of her, providing her with soaking relief. The birth mark on his quad she always kissed before taking his hard length in her mouth, savoring his taste. The buzz cut of his black hair buried between her thighs, his mouth lavishing her once again. Then his smooth almond skin was under hers while he sat up, wrapping his lips over her nipple, sucking moans from them both. His strong hands gripped her ass, riding her down hard over his cock, always delivering a gushing orgasm for both through gasps of love.

Then… he was gone.

Charlie's love. Gone. Her safety. Gone. Her future. Gone. And sometimes—in her weakest moments when it all flashed back, she feared—her sanity. Gone too.

The memory held such pleasure for her. And pain. A pain that lumped in her throat.

She didn't want to fuck anymore. She wanted to hide, safe and alone, either at home or working in the shadows of a set, guarding other women who needed her protection from threats. Threats like what Charlie had already survived.

That's why she did this. The job protecting Juliette became her saving grace. When she focused on another woman's safety, she didn't have to be concerned for her own.

Because Charlie was still at risk. Her instinct rose every day with the dawn to warn her. It hovered over her like the moon in the day sky. Promising her…

It will come back for you, Charlie Girl. It doesn't matter why you did it. Karma will find you. You will pay the price one day.

Lindy approached her with dark hair hanging wet, a white towel wrapped around her dripping body. She had been generous to Juliette. Charlie heard the two women's tongues and fingers thrill each other for almost an hour. She saw how their bodies twisted with release while the two men enjoyed each other, turning their gaze often, admiring the mutual show of pleasure.

"Mind if I join you?" Lindy's steps neared like a curious deer, mouth barely confessing, "I think I may be done for the night."

It tensed Charlie's shoulders. Not for the almost nude woman closing in. Charlie tensed to the distraction Lindy tried to impose over her watch of Juliette. Bodies were moving in water. Juliette's petite brunette form was between two towering men. "Not at all," Charlie said, her eyes on Juliette while wary of the woman sitting down beside her on the sofa.

But all was fine.

Juliette was entering another heavenly world by her view. Sitting on the edge of the Jacuzzi, Martin put her on his lap with her back to his chest, her legs spread wide and draped over his thighs. His condom-sheathed cock started fucking her from behind while Santiago knelt between Juliette's legs, his mouth indulging her clit.

Damn, lucky woman, Charlie grinned for her friend. Wishing she had a champagne flute to raise for her. A penis cake lit with sparkling candles. A big-ass, red-lip balloon bouquet hanging over her bed. They would surely be laughing about this adventure for years to come.

"She's super nice," Lindy quietly said, both with eyes on Juliette. "I was star struck by her at first, but then she talked to me, and she seemed so real, so kind."

"She is very kind." It made Charlie grin. "And very real."

The contrast of Charlie's career against Juliette's struck her then. Like they worked in opposite worlds. Juliette's? It was one of fiction. But the emotions she brought to it? They were very real. And Charlie's world? It was as real as death any next moment. So, you brought no emotions to it. You stayed numb and you stayed alive. Or at least... you tried. Either way. The opposition matched them like puzzle pieces—a perfect, close, friendly fit.

"How long have you done this?" Lindy asked, turning the focus on Charlie rather than the salacious show in front of them.

"Done what?"

"Protected women like this?"

"Guess you could say 'bout seven years."

"Do you always protect famous women?"

"No."

Lindy sat on Charlie's right. And even though Charlie's eyes carefully watched Juliette, refusing to be distracted by the woman, she knew Lindy was highly distracted with what was in her line of sight—the long, jagged scar across Charlie's right cheek.

She nodded right toward it. "Did you get that protecting women?"

Wow, Charlie Girl. Guess this woman ain't so mousy after all. Having a foursome and asking a complete stranger about a scar on her face? That takes ovaries.

Charlie started to like her. It forced honesty out of her mouth. "I got it protecting two girls."

Flashes of little hands and a flak vest. Sounds of gunshots. Smells of bread and dirt. The metallic taste of blood. Painful memories shot through Charlie's mind. She squeezed her eyes shut to stop them. "And I'd do it all again but need to end this conversation right now."

That was the only thing that could distract Charlie… to a dangerous degree.

When that memory threatened, she lost all time and place. So, she pushed it and everything away to stay safe, to keep Juliette safe. And her.

"Sorry. I didn't mean to upset you." Lindy turned her profile to the stars above. "I can just read people. Read their energy, their auras. Yours is off the charts with indigo. I've been watching you all night. It kept calling to me. I couldn't look away from you." On cue, her regard bounced back to Charlie's profile.

Breath huffed from Charlie's lungs. She didn't know how much of that notion she believed. She did meditate. She did know the power of a trained mind over the body, especially one in pain. And Charlie did know the power she had herself to see what wasn't there… yet. To sense danger coming from miles away, years even.

Maybe it wasn't bullshit.

"What does indigo mean?" Charlie asked, eyes still on Juliette who was moaning with her own aura of ecstasy. Martin was pinching her nipples, making her grind down on his cock while Santiago lapped up the lust between their thighs with his ambitious mouth sucking her clit, then traveling his tongue down Martin's shaft fucking her, then back up again to thrill Juliette.

"Indigo is intuitive. You guide people. You're good at calculating risk."

Holy shit. That insight almost turned her attention toward the eerie wisdom coming from the woman's mouth.

But then again, wasn't that obvious?

She sat right there, guiding the night to one of no risk while she protected a famous woman currently fucking two men at one time. No major cosmic revelations. Only orgasms and shouts.

"I can see black and white swirling in your aura too." The tone in Lindy's voice lowered. "Black means pain or grief, and white means protection."

Those sudden words threatened to strangle the fact lumping in Charlie's throat. She swallowed it down, clenching her jaw before she said, "You can see the truth, Lindy."

"What happened?"

"I can't talk about it."

"Because of the pain?"

"Because it's a secret."

A secret that Charlie would not speak of. Only to a few. Like Juliette. Like Rob. They found out when they weren't supposed to. They saw it written down Charlie's naked, scarred body. And they witnessed how it's written across her scarred mind too, a mind she can't always control if she drops her guard. It's a secret of rules broken that breaks Charlie's psyche when the truth comes flooding back.

"You're American?" The woman's questions sat beside

Charlie. Not threatening.

She'd indulge them. "Yes. And you're what? Australian?"

"My accent is obvious. So is yours. Southern right? From Texas?"

It always amused Charlie. To non-Americans, all Southerners were from Texas. Far from it. Literally. "No. I'm from South Carolina."

"There's energy all around you. You're not alone. You're from a loving family. And you're married, aren't you?"

The energy around Charlie wasn't married. Not anymore. It was buried. Along with family she loved. "No, I'm not married. Don't have a family. I'm alone." Charlie's sight still aimed at Juliette. And Martin. He was motioning for them to move to the lush bed just inside the open glass doors. "What about you and Martin? How long have you two been together?"

The skill was ingrained in Charlie—give just enough intel to get some.

Her turn now.

"A few weeks. I'm hostel hopping my way around the world and he's living off his Dutch mother's trust fund. She's some kind of famous judge in the International Criminal Court at The Hague. So, he's running from his mum's strict rule. I met him in Malta at a bar and he suggested Ibiza next."

"What about Santiago?" Charlie scored the information she craved, nodding toward the two men, one whose hard cock was hovering in front Juliette's mouth while the other one was entering her, making her moan from behind. Charlie's body shifted toward the open bedroom door where she was ready to strike if at any time Juliette's pleasure turned into pain she didn't want.

"We met Santiago a couple nights ago here in Ibiza at a club." Lindy stood up. "He's local. And a model shooting something here at this hotel. Can't you tell?"

Hell yes, Charlie Girl. You can tell.

Tell by the tapered sex line of Santiago's carved obliques thrusting his impressive cock into Juliette's pussy. Tell by his bicep tensing with his hold around Juliette's waist while his other long arm reached around, playing her clit. Santiago was model indeed, making Juliette groan like a wild animal with each thrust that put her mouth deeper down Martin's cock. Her shaking thighs, eyes rolling back in a sudden, seized silence revealed another shuddering orgasm he was delivering to her.

"Those two are all for her now." Lindy took steps toward the bedroom. "I'm going to grab a shower."

"Hey, Lindy." Charlie's quiet call stopped the kind woman's steps, turning her back to face Charlie. "Is Martin good to you? Does he ever hurt you?"

It didn't matter how much pleasure the man was giving and receiving, Charlie couldn't shake it. She could see right past his blond, Dutch beauty... and saw something hiding. Something waiting to hurt, waiting to harm someone.

"No. But he's intense. I guess that's what makes me nervous around him sometimes. I can't quite put my finger on it. But he's hot and rich. And he likes sharing his drugs. They help me relax and sleep. Guess you could say I have my own secrets and pain I need to escape too."

The words stopped Charlie's heart. She knew what the

woman had just shared with her. *That* secret. *That* pain all too many women had known.

It put Charlie's eyes on her now, compassionate eyes that couldn't help it. Charlie would protect her too.

"Just be careful with him, Lindy. Martin isn't who you think he is. Trust me. I can read his aura too."

FIVE

●

Charlie offered wisdom and a tall glass of water to Juliette standing beside her, naked and proud. "You better drink all this water and go piss like a Russian racehorse or you're gonna have a urinary tract infection from hell."

It was three a.m. and three bodies slept in Juliette's bed. Charlie stood in the living room by the little bar, brewing coffee while keeping an eye on the door to Juliette's bedroom. It was wide open.

"It would be worth it." Juliette took the full glass but didn't wipe the smile from her face. "Oh my God, Charlie. I can't even tell you how fucking good that was. It's like once I said 'yes', once we started, there was no going back. I just wanted more. Like I kissed three pairs of lips and kissed all shame goodbye. I just let myself indulge in tongues, fingers, pussies and cocks everywhere. Fucking hell, I will live fantasizing about this night for years to come. Literally. I've never come so many times. I lost count at six orgasms."

"Hell, I lost count at six condoms." Charlie stretched her arms over head. "Those men must be poppin' some blue pills."

Charlie had just checked on Rob. He was sitting in a white lounge chair outside the suite door, playing on his tablet. Neither shock nor shame was on his face for their assignment tonight either. He would surely be giving Juliette high-fives for this too.

"What are we doing next?" Charlie asked Juliette, watching her gulp down the glass of water. "Are we kicking them out or are you going in for another round?"

Just then a silhouette appeared in the bedroom doorway. The sexy one that started this whole X-rated escapade.

Santiago propositioned Juliette. "Care to shower with me?"

Damn that man and his tempting invitations. Seems they could convince Juliette to run naked through Piccadilly Circus, paparazzi and all. Charlie just hoped the woman didn't lose her mind *and* heart to him.

Juliette reached her hand out. He stepped to where she beckoned and took it while Juliette asked her, "Mind if we use your bathroom? I don't want to wake our other guests."

More like Juliette wanted Santiago all to herself. Charlie didn't blame her. "Sure," she said, stepping aside so they could cross to her room.

"We won't be waking them up." Santiago informed them, enticed in Juliette's direction, toward Charlie's empty bedroom. "Lindy took something. She's out. And Martin is snoring like a mule."

"You two go have fun." Charlie turned to pour cups

of coffee for herself and Rob. "Just don't use all my body soap."

Santiago's voice cooed from the threshold to Charlie's bedroom. "Sure we can't convince you to join us?"

It turned her gaze back to him with a smile. "You sure are a glutton for rejection, Santiago. I already said no once."

"I'm a glutton for the rare occasion of two women like you in one night. I heard you by the pool today. I'm game. I'd be a lucky mechanical bull to have a famous, stunning beauty and a secret, sexy badass ride me. You can't blame a man for trying for both."

"Try all you want; I don't fuck on the job."

Juliette's voice chimed in from the bedroom, overhearing the exchange. "Charlie, you don't fuck at all. But it will be my job one day to see that you do."

Charlie called back to her, "You stick to acting and I'll stick to ass-kicking, bitch, and we'll both be just fine." She made them all laugh. But when Santiago reached to close the bedroom door behind him Charlie said, "Uh-uh. It stays open. Never block my access to protect my mark."

With a soft salute, Santiago obeyed, turning like a horny puppy, following Juliette to their next fucking destination.

Charlie opened the suite door with a hot cup of coffee in her hand, offering it to Rob. "Hey fucker, have some jolt juice."

"Thanks, fucker." Winking, he reached up for the cup. "I heard the tempting offer in there. Was wondering if you really meant it. You would never, under any circumstance, fuck on the job?"

"Why? You finally offerin'?" She stood in the doorway... feeling the huge smile and joke between them.

"I stand beside your hot ass all day and I've seen you naked. You're fucking gorgeous, Ravenel, but you're my colleague and not my type."

"My loss." She and Rob were close. Very close after what he did for her in L.A. when they were recruited. And once again what he did for her in London too. That was their secret. And their bond. One they would always protect. "Besides, *I* don't have a type anymore."

"Oh, I bet I could find a type to change your stubborn mind." Rob lifted his screen up to inches from her face. "Like this one. He won't get the fuck out of my feed."

An image of the most heart-stopping man Charlie had ever seen, hell the world had seen, smoldered back at her from the device.

The shot?

It was a magazine cover featuring a massive, shredded torso straining under a thin, wet, white T-shirt. A black tendril fell in front of aqua eyes that reached out from any dimension to right between her thighs. The perfection of his masculine face—almost humanly impossible. That's why the cover headline for the actor cast for the blockbuster *Zeus* movies read, "DANIEL PIERCE IS A SEXY GOD."

Damn, Charlie Girl. The sight of the man suddenly flashed a distant feeling across her heart. Something about him. It summoned her like a lightning storm over a dark ocean, watching its magnificent approach, one that would surely flood her world wet.

Still, she said to Rob, "Sexy, arrogant, A-list celebrities are not my type. Never."

Rob shook his head, lowering the tablet, taunting her. "You promised me to never say never, Ravenel."

Her eyes rolled but her lips smiled at his persistence. "Whatever. I'm going back to work, Vasquez." She closed the wooden door behind her.

Pulling one of the white chairs into the middle of the living room, she sat so she could watch both bedrooms. The vantage point gave her surveillance over the bodies sleeping on Juliette's bed to her left, and to her right, to her bed, still made and empty with an occupied bathroom beyond it.

The night sky and soft lull of ocean waves were behind her while Juliette's soft giggles from the shower filled the rest of the air. The plastic of the chair was cool against Charlie's jeans, but the coffee poised under her mouth was hot. Air blew over her lips, over the dark steaming liquid before her first sip.

The raw flush from the picture of that actor kept lapping her mind. It swirled with the sultry night, tempting her to walk memory lane again. To a honeymoon night on the bed with him, with Kai pouring warm oil down her back, kneeling behind her, spreading the oil with his hands, spreading her legs with his knees, massaging down to her crevice, getting ready to…

Movement to her left.

Stirring on Juliette's bed.

Glowing uplights from the balcony and the moon outside poured in enough light through the wall of windows into the bedroom for Charlie to witness...

Martin sat up. He stretched his arms wide before sneaking both hands between his legs under the sheets. He looked around the bed. Looked over to Lindy's body beside him. He nudged her leg hard with his elbow. She didn't respond. He did it again. Her passive body only bobbed back against his shove.

Charlie had no idea what the woman had taken but it was obvious—Lindy was out cold.

That's why what happened next had Charlie's pulse climbing, muscles arching, heat firing across her nerves.

Martin rose to kneel over the passed-out woman, jerking his hardening cock off over her vulnerable body. A body unable to give consent, unable to refuse what it didn't want. Breath heaved from Martin's lungs with intent to take, to harm her, to climax to it all.

Charlie gently set her coffee cup down on the marble floor beside her, fingers next snagging the laces tight on her tactical boots before she sat back up. It made her sick knowing where he thought this was going.

Hell-to-the-never, Charlie Girl. Not on your watch.

She stood up. Her steps quietly approached the bedroom while Martin knelt oblivious to her approach. He pulled the sheet back from Lindy's naked body. With one hand, he spread her thighs open to prepare for his assault while his other kept jerking him off.

"Don't even fucking think about it." Charlie barked at him from steps away.

"Think about it?" He turned, evil lechery and violence firing across his eyes. The yank of his cock only grew faster for the defenseless woman and to Charlie's command, pre-cum dripping at their confrontation. "I do more than think about it. I do it all the time. They love it. It gives them the best dreams. Me too. Watch."

"Leave her alone. Get the fuck up. Walk out the door. And look over your shoulder for the rest of your life because I swear, I will fucking kill men like you. I already have."

The stroke of his cock trembled even faster, milking the tip. The sick fuck was getting off on getting caught. Quickly. "I've been craving this, planning this all night—her compliance and your resistance. Want to come touch me? To try to stop me?"

"Now that's how you ask a lady." Her words blasted along with her right booted foot, kicking it up to strike his tender belly, making his arms flail open at the air knocked from his lungs. Charlie grabbed his right arm, torquing it so hard against his shoulder joint it forced him back. He fell off the bed, but she didn't let go, their bodies landing in a crunch to the floor.

With a lightning coil, she wrapped her legs around his neck, his right arm still in her grasp. Trapping it high between her squeezing thighs, she forced his shoulder into a painful, unnatural, compliant hold, forcing shouts of agony from his throat.

Their crashing struggle and Martin's screams rushed Rob through the door. Charlie heard him slam it open. Heard his heavy boots running their way. Heard his huffing breath covering her back.

"Sup, fucker," she said, smiling up at Rob. He stood

above her while the asshole between her legs kept crying out at the pain she inflicted with glee.

SIX

Lindy sat on the sofa in her minidress. She picked at a scab on her arm. "I didn't know he was doing that." Dawn light filled the sitting room of the suite while her fingernails ripped dried blood from her flesh, her eyes registering the shock of the violation. "I didn't know he was fucking me while I was passed out."

"That's called rape," Charlie said.

"But we have sex all the time when I'm awake and I don't say no."

"Just because you invite a guest into your home when you're awake, doesn't mean they can break and enter later when you aren't there, when you're drunk or when you're asleep," Charlie replied. "It's a fucking crime, he's a sick son-of-a-bitch, and I'm itching to put three bullets through him."

Charlie glanced over at Martin on his knees.

Rob had him secured in the bedroom, his wrists bound in zip-tie handcuffs behind his back, torqued back so tight, making Martin groan at the pain Charlie introduced to his now-dislocated shoulder. Rob was investigating him, scrolling through Martin's phone, waiting for their next move.

"I had no idea he was doing this." Santiago sat next to Juliette on the sofa, his face twisting with fear and disgust he would be guilty by association. "I swear. We only just met, and he seemed nice, charming even and very generous."

Charlie said, "They usually are when you first meet them. They overwhelm you with affection, distracting you so their evil can sneak in unnoticed."

Charlie glanced over at Juliette. She was in shock too.

Charlie asked, "What do y'all wanna do?" This was Lindy's call and Juliette would support it, Charlie knew. But it would rain a shit storm of horrific press into Juliette's celebrity world. "Rob has Martin's phone unlocked. He's found all sorts of photos of women he's raped like this."

"But you can't prove it without knowing their names and getting sworn statements." Juliette shook her head with wisdom, with an experience Charlie already knew about. Juliette was all too aware of how this works, all too familiar with the lack of justice.

Juliette continued, her lip curling up in disgust, "And even then, people want to believe the man and blame the woman. Because they don't want to accept that they're also at risk, that no matter what they do, this can happen to them or someone they love. Until it does."

"I don't want the police involved." Lindy chimed in, dragging her fingers through her dark strands. "I have my own life I'm running from. I don't need the scrutiny or the publicity."

"I'll support you, Lindy," Juliette said. "I will stand in it with you and fight if that's what you want to do. I have the money for the best lawyers. We can try for justice."

That's the Juliette Jones that Charlie loved.

If the world thought the celebrity on the screen was warm, beautiful and loving, they had no idea. This was a woman willing to ruin her career to defend another.

It was another reason why Charlie loved Juliette so much. Another way they were exactly alike.

"Thank you." Lindy reached her hand out to squeeze Juliette's beside her. "But I mean it. I can't get involved with the police. I've got drug possession charges against me. Drugs I use to forget shit like this. And I know you mean the best, but with you around, the publicity would be life-ruining… for us both." She closed her eyes, almost in prayer and said, "I trust Martin will get his own justice one day."

Charlie slapped her hands over her black-jeaned knees, standing up, resolved. "Damn right, he will." She headed into the bedroom to consult with Rob.

"Sup, fucker." He glanced up from dropping the photos from Martin's phone onto his HGR laptop, securing the evidence. Going through Martin's laptop that he had found in his rucksack too, Rob documented all his crimes—what he found on the devices, in the cloud and online. Once that proof was locked down, Rob would delete all he could before confiscating both, preventing any further harm done to these women by more photos sold or made public.

Charlie stood in constant awe of Rob's tech skills. Though he looked like a linebacker, really, he was a nerd who loved anything with computers. "What's our next move?" he asked, clicking away on his keyboard.

She sucked her teeth, aiming for justice they couldn't have. Lindy wouldn't press charges. She understood why. But Charlie could think of one woman who may bestow her own kind of justice. *If* she was the kind of woman Charlie hoped she would be.

"Does his phone have a contact name for his mom?"

The audible groan from Martin to Charlie's question wasn't from the pain in his shoulder. It was her answer. Yes, his mother would be enraged to know what her own son had done. Maybe that would stop him. It definitely would stop the money funding his violent visits across the globe.

Charlie squatted down in front of her victim, relishing his agony. "What do you think your mother, the judge in The Hague who has issued sentences over global violence against women will do once I show her the evidence of the rapist you are? Her very own son?"

Martin lifted his eyes to Charlie. They were beaten and afraid. His lips, not responding.

"You've got an answer in your mouth and another shoulder I can permanently fuck up too if you don't say it."

She waited. She always could—for minutes, hours, years—to get what she wanted. But it didn't take long. Not when she put her index finger against his right shoulder and pushed firm against swollen tissue and bone bent back to where it didn't belong.

"Face the truth now, Martin, or it will haunt you for the

rest of your life."

"Argh!" He wrenched back at her pain and promise. Mouth trembling, shaking at the torture. "She will destroy me."

"I like her already."

Charlie stood up. She took Martin's phone from Rob and walked out to the balcony to seal the rapist's fate. Hoping. Trusting. That if justice didn't come from the law, it would come from a mom.

It was a conversation of mutual respect. One between a woman who had fought, boots on the ground, to help other women. And another who fought from behind the bench to do the same. It filled Charlie with faith, once again, in that strong force. The mother went from shock, to fury, to focused action in doling out justice against her own son. Some way for sure, she promised, she would do all she could such that her son would never hurt another.

Just in case, Charlie placed another call after she ended that one.

"Hey, boss." Her vision took in the Mediterranean and the orange orb rising above it. But her mind conjured a man, sitting in his London office, ready to deploy any back-up or justice she and Rob called for.

"Ravenel, rough life being paid to visit exotic locations, sitting by the pool, and soaking up the rays, yeah?"

"Yeah, twelve hours standing in a dark stage building on set or behind a cast chair under a pop-up tent on a cold, wet England morning is real fucking exotic."

She had only worked for Jeremy, the head of HGR Security, for a year and already loved his no bullshit ways and unwavering support.

Once she filled him in on their current detail, location and the events of the night before, Jeremy clicked his pen. Charlie recognized the sound in her ear, the sound of his tell. He was pissed… and ready to act.

"Send me a copy of his passport and we will sort it from here," he said. "Between his mum and our agents in the Netherlands, we can watch him."

"I've known men like him." Her eyes to the horizon, the sun rose along with her instinct. "He will try again. He'll try to hurt another woman."

"We'll do all we can. I don't doubt your instinct. It's what I hired you for. That and your fight. Your smart-arse mouth is just a bonus."

He made her smile and reply, "Careful what you pay me for, boss."

"The only ones who need to be careful are the men you aim for, Ravenel."

Officially, that was true.

SEVEN

🌙

The mattress sank beside her. Sheets rustled to her right. A perfume of bergamot and violets filled the air next to her.

"Is this a slumber party?" Charlie asked, cracking her exhausted eyelids open to the noon light and Juliette climbing into her bed, resting her head on the pillow next to her.

"Yes." Juliette tucked a hand under her cheek. "Just because you're not ready to take a man to bed yet doesn't mean you have to suffer and sleep alone."

The comment hit so close it almost snuck tears over Charlie's tired lashes. Because no matter how raw and ragged she felt after that morning, she still couldn't sleep. Even when she did, with pillows in a nest all around her, they were no comfort against the nightmares that visited like ghosts.

Reaching her hand out, she held Juliette's in hers between the pillows. "You and Rob are the only ones welcome in my bed."

"Fucking lucky we are then." Juliette wore a warm smile before a pinch of worry crinkled across her eyebrows. "You're not leaving me now, leaving my detail, are you?"

"Why would you think that?"

"I know it's been a lot with me. Like last night. Bloody hell, since the first day you were on this job, you've had to fight for me."

"That first day was just a warning to a Sound Assistant getting a little handsy putting your mic pack on."

"You were right though. He was a creep who took too long with clipping the pack to my bra. You intimidated us both that day."

"I intimidated you?"

"Charlie, your stare could ice the Sahara Desert. But then when you grabbed Maltesers from Craft Services and started tossing them in your mouth like popcorn, I knew you were all heart and jolly underneath."

"Yeah, and when you danced around on set to the Bee Gees with no fear of ridicule, I knew you weren't uppity… just plumb crazy."

"No, it was this morning that was crazy." Juliette's gaze traveled from Charlie's scarred cheek to her bare right shoulder, to the scar of the bullet shot through it. "I'm so sorry, love. I should've listened to your instinct. My crazy fun got us into this sodding mess."

"No, it helped us catch a rapist. Fair trade."

"But it's got to be hard on you. Fighting another man like that. One like Martin."

"Actually…" Charlie audited the rush of emotion that floods her in those moments. No hesitant fear, only focused fury. "—it's shockingly easy. The only thing that hurts me is the harm that comes to others, not to me."

"Still, Charlie." Juliette lifted a lock of hair off Charlie's cheek, resting it back behind her. "I know you suffer sometimes. I see it written all over your beautiful face. I love it when you laugh and joke with me, but a woman knows another's pain, recognizes it when it's resting right beside her." Her hand gave a little squeeze to hers. "You miss him, don't you?"

"What's scary, Jules, is that I'm missing him less and less, with each passing month. And I feel guilty about it. Guilty that I'm still here, alive, starting to have fun again, starting a new life without him. And he's forever gone. And I'm the asshole moving on."

"From what you've told me about Kai, he would have wanted you to move on. The man sounds as lovely as he looked in the photos you showed me. He wouldn't want you living on in guilt."

Charlie shuffled from her stomach to her side. Grateful for yet another friendship where honesty was brutal and beautiful at the same time.

"Kai couldn't get me to do anything either," she said. "I'm stubborn through and through. I don't think I'll ever stop feeling guilty when I think about him."

Juliette mirrored her, turning her naked torso toward Charlie's in a tank and panties. "Then what's your favorite memory of him? Try remembering the good stuff when you think about him. At least don't have guilt about that."

"There's too many to pick just one."

"Try. Just focus on something wonderful about him."

"Wonderful? Well... he was confident and sexy in a subtle way."

"Oh." A delighted smile landed on Juliette's face. "Subtle, sexy and confident? Do tell. How?"

"Like the first time we kissed." The memory played in her mind. It put a grin on her face. "He was my first everything. I think I intimidated guys away, but not him. For our first three dates, we just held hands and good God, I wanted to kiss him. I wanted to do much more with him, but I was so shy back then."

"You? Shy? I can't imagine it."

"Well, hell. I was nineteen. I felt like an awkward freak because I'd never been kissed, like something was wrong with me."

"Nothing is wrong with you, my sweet."

Charlie loved this. Not the generous compliments from her friend. It was the intimacy. The vulnerable moments. A life on guard left her craving any time when she could drop hers and show herself. The trouble was, after everything, after so long... she struggled to remember who that woman was.

"He took me hiking on our fourth date." Charlie settled into her spot on the bed and smiled even bigger. "We got to the summit. He held my hand and asked me if I had another piece of gum. I was chewing one but didn't bring more with me. I told him so and he asked if he could share mine.

"When I said 'yes', I was so nervous. I knew what he meant. But he took my face in his hands and gently kissed me, taking minutes upon minutes of just his lips exploring mine until finally giving me a little tongue. Fuck, he turned me on. So patient. So sexy. Slowly giving me more and more. Kissing me like he was telling how he would fuck me our first time. It was like we kissed forever and when he finally pulled away, he had my gum in his mouth. Then he nuzzled his nose against mine and joked how he loved cinnamon too."

"I'm so jealous." Juliette's face twisted with sweet regret. "I was thirteen and Henry Williams was my first French kiss. It was like getting my teeth flossed by his tongue. Then he was my first bonk at sixteen, my first five seconds of nothing special."

"I guess me waiting a bit made it so much better," Charlie said. "Then it was like I opened a bag of potato chips and couldn't eat just one. I devoured the man after that first kiss. Damn how I made up for lost time." Time, she recalled that became marriage at twenty-two, one full of love but with a rushed ceremony before they were sent to war.

Juliette's eyebrows raised an inch. "You were eating him like crisps? Go on then. Tell me. What's your sexiest memory?"

If Charlie let herself do this, to only remember the bliss and let go of the pain, happiness did find her. Should she do this more often? Maybe it would finally ease the grief so she could possibly move on. Hoping to love again felt too bold, too greedy. But please, maybe at least another hot fuck. Or hell, even just a kiss.

"I remember the first time he made me come."

"Oh yes, bitch. I want that story. How old were you?"

"Twenty. We went camping by Navajo Lake. We'd just gone swimming and were in our tent. He was fingering me, but I couldn't come. It had frustrated us both for a year. So, he sat up, nude, hard and hot as hell, asking me to show him how I do it to myself. At first, I was shy, but I trusted him so much that I tried. He watched me, and it started turning us both on. So fucking much. Then his fingers joined mine, learning how to do it. He got so good at it that within minutes I would be drenching his hand."

Juliette grinned, no judgement in her expression, only delight. "You're giving me ideas for tonight." Her ideas—Santiago and Lindy—were at Santiago's apartment, showering, napping and planning to rejoin Juliette later for dinner.

"Yeah, well you'll enjoy this part."

Charlie piled more on top of her sweet, sexy story; her heart singing to only think about love. "It became Kai's little kink with me. He begged me to finger myself while he drove. While cars and trunks went right past us and could maybe see me. If we had the road to ourselves, he'd reach over and help me finish."

"Charlie, that is too hot. You can't tell me that you don't want that again. With someone, someday."

Juliette's grip pulled the sheet up to snuggle under her chin, like she was cozying up to the promise of a future full of love and sex for her best friend. "You can have any man," she said. "I see how they come on to you. You're like catnip even though you push them away. It only turns them on more."

"I'm not playing games with them, Jules. I push men away for a reason."

"I know. But you're too loving, too incredible to be

alone forever. I won't allow it. Can't you just share your body and keep your heart? At least for a night?"

"Jules." The truth broke the dam holding back her tears. "I don't know if I could ever let go again and relax. If I can ever be with another man. I'd be too worried about what he was thinking."

They fell over her lashes while she lifted the sheet with her right arm, the scars on her cheek and shoulder already revealed, she uncovered the brutal one above her right hip bone.

"Who wants to fuck a body while looking at these?" Charlie asked. "I can hardly look at them myself. It'll only bring it all back for me. Who wants to suffer through that?"

More tears fell. Charlie bit her lip, holding back a sob that threatened her with fear. Fear that it was true, that she would forever be alone. No, that she *had* to be alone.

"Charlie…" The break in Juliette's tone and face joined her at the bottom of her fear. "—you're beautiful. Your scars are beautiful. They're your story. One you should bloody well be proud of and never ashamed about. Any man would be fucking lucky and humbled to have you."

"That's easy for you to say. You're perfection in the flesh and on the screen, every square inch of you."

"No, I'm not. You know that. I've got scars you can't see. Ones that fuck with my mind too." The grip over the sheet in Juliette's hand tightened. "But I swore to myself long ago, though it happened to me, I would never let it define me. That I would enjoy life. And sex. No one can take that away from me."

Taken away? So much had been from Charlie. The loss

started to piss her off. Why couldn't she get some of it back? God knows she had the stubborn will to get anything she wanted.

The problem is… what do you want, Charlie Girl? Love or safety? Because you can't have both. You'll have to decide one day.

"I promise—" She swore to Juliette. And herself. "…that I'll try *if* I ever meet someone worth fucking my life sideways for."

It was a promise she made free of guilt because it would never happen. No one would ever be worth risking it all.

"Agreed," Juliette said. "They shall require my full inspection."

"Bitch, I don't want your sloppy seconds."

They both smiled through tears. "I'm fucking my way across Ibiza, not London," Juliette said. "That leaves plenty of men for you to have all to yourself."

The tip of Charlie's finger flitted down Juliette's nose, playing. "Maybe one day. But I think I'll start with just wearing a bikini in public. Then maybe with just fucking one man. Not two and a woman… all night long."

That tossed Juliette's little chin up in laughter, eyes dancing in the memory already. "Oh, my love, you'll catch up with me one day."

"For now." Charlie snuggled the sheet up under her too. "Let's catch up on some sleep. You need rest for round two. Or wait. I mean seven. Or are you ready for sixty-nine now?"

That had them rolling, sharing a few more sultry details until both finally tapped out, closing their eyes, contended grins on their faces lying side by side.

Charlie's hand reached out to hold Juliette's while they slept.

She may have lost everything, but friendships she still had. That crept a happy tear over her lashes.

EIGHT

A lightness filled Charlie's muscles. Her shoulders fell, relaxed. A curve kept taking her lips in a soft smile with a serene pleasure soothing across her nerves. She could almost feel guilty about what she did if it hadn't have felt... so... damn... good.

The knock at the hotel door didn't even make her jump. Right on time. Eight p.m. One glance through the peephole and she opened it.

"Sup, fucker." Rob's grin reliably greeted her. His eyes dropped to the book in her hand. "I see it's your typical night off."

"I'm working on her, love." Juliette's voice neared from behind Charlie. "You should've heard the steamy stories she told me today. One day, I'm sure, she'll put down the books and make up for lost time."

"Oh yeah?" Rob asked. "What steamy stories did she tell?"

"I'm standing right here, fuckers." Charlie's free hand held the door for Juliette while Rob secured the hallway.

"Come on," she said. "We're all hungry for a little something in our mouths tonight... whatever that may be."

The threesome took their usual formation in the breezeway from Juliette and Charlie's suite out to the hotel courtyard rimmed with flowers blooming abundant. Charlie took advance position while Rob secured their backs.

"Oh!" Juliette stumbled. "Bloody ribbon." She knelt to better secure her platform espadrilles to her ankle with their wraparound bow.

The moment gave Charlie and Rob pause. One, to hold position. Two, for Rob to scrutinize Charlie's face like a treasure map looking for gold.

"You're glowing, mi prima," he said to her. "And fucking smiling. What the hell happened this afternoon? I thought you two were just taking naps and telling stories."

His deft observation sent a shock of blush up Charlie's cheeks, feeling the busted heat rise from her neck up to the tips of her ears.

"We did," Juliette reported without looking up, snagging the white ribbon tighter.

"Uh-huh." Half of Rob's face cocked in a smile. "Tell that to Charlie's face. She did something else today too. She's fucking radiant with sin."

Charlie couldn't help it. "Shut up, fucker." A delighted squirm took her entire body, shaking her head, guilty, not even able to look at him.

Rob's laughter filled the breezeway before the bass of his voice sounded off. "Holy shit. I did find your type, didn't I?"

Fuck yes, he did. And Charlie stood there, body glowing,

not knowing if she should swim in the pleasure or the guilt of it.

That afternoon, while Juliette had disappeared into her shower, Charlie took her own. At first, the mundane ritual was mindless to her until she stood under the nozzle, rinsing conditioner from her hair. Little rivers of warm water tickling over her nipples greeted the cool air around her. The sensation woke her body.

That body woke a mind that remembered what her chat with Juliette had inspired—all the sexy memories with her husband Charlie could recall in vivid detail. Those would usually send her fingers searching for her little vibrator, playing with herself in bed, indulging memories from years before.

But not that afternoon. She was too tired. Tired of living in grief. Tired of living in the past. Closing her eyes, she let it wash away, breathing in only the present moment.

One that had her swirling her fingertips over her nipples, gently twirling and pulling until pleasure radiated like lightning between her thighs. She held a hand there, secure in that thrill while the other descended between her legs. Touching sensitive skin that almost hurt with ache, with need. Sliding down through her wet folds, no memories, no past this time. Only breath, steam, warm water and hands lavishing her body too.

Then the quickening had happened, her breath, drawing more and more shallow. Thoughts of a shredded torso under a white T-shirt with a wet body like hers had inspired it. A black tendril over aqua eyes that she had conjured, the tempo of her fingers took her to only that new vision. One that had reached from the screen to between her thighs, like her hand was then, palm grinding down over her clit, fingers plunging inside.

Leaning back against the cool tile, she let it. Let her imagination and that sight of him rain over her. No past pain. No present torment. Only an overwhelming torrent of pleasure that had her trembling with a powerful release she'd never felt. So much pouring from her, crying out in pleasure, crying out in joy, crying to let go of so much with a sigh of a name she didn't even know.

The erotic memory had her suddenly huffing for breath, running back to the present moment with Rob's eyes witnessing the delicious flush across her face at the sudden race.

He grinned at her spectacle. "Told you to never say never, mi prima."

"What are you two going on about?" Juliette stood up. Shoe emergency resolved.

"Nothing," Charlie said while Rob's words thundered over them with, "Daniel Pierce."

"Daniel Pierce? We did a flop of a movie together years ago." Juliette's brow creased confused. "Why? Is he here?"

"No," Rob said. "But after his picture that I showed to Charlie last night, he's in her horny little head." The twinkle in Rob's eyes was pure satisfaction. Like her solo pleasure was the biggest fish he could hook on his line... for now.

"No, he's not." The lie even tasted like bullshit in Charlie's mouth. "All this fucking around me just finally gave me a few minutes to fuck myself. Stick to your fantasies, Vasquez, and I'll stick to mine."

"Daniel Pierce is every one's fantasy," Juliette said. "I would've let him roger me, but I don't fuck on the job. And he was too busy fucking others on set. He had no time for me."

"See, Vasquez." Charlie found the ammo to go on offense. "It's like I always say, you men get to fuck like rabbits, even at work, while us women have to keep it in our pants, or we lose our careers."

His hands went up in mock surrender. "I know it's bullshit. I see it around me all the time. It's why mine stays in my pants at work too. I'm just glad to see you smiling so big, mi prima."

She gave him a wink. Really? She had no shame around Rob or Juliette. Certainly not about sex. It was just the strange feeling that unnerved her. She wasn't sad. She was happy. And a little horny. And it wasn't from memories. It was from the vast unknown of a future she fought like hell to have, one that afternoon she had dared to imagine.

"Well, I'm glad to see you both smiling." Juliette's steps continued their path toward the patio restaurant, toward what awaited her that night. "I'm going to miss you two when we wrap. I'll be so bloody bored without you."

"No, you won't," Rob said. "You're coming on vacation with me and Charlie."

"Holiday with you two?" Juliette's voice rang out. "Hell yes."

The change of plans lifted Charlie's spirits even higher. "Oh god help us then," she said. "With both y'all unleashed on that Caribbean island, nothing will be staying in anyone's pants."

Their path halted.

"Speaking of," Juliette said.

Santiago and Lindy stood before them, waiting at the empty bar, wine glasses in hand, eager smiles on their face... ready for Juliette and whatever the hell round they were on now.

NINE

☾

"Alone, tonight?"

A deep voice in a lush accent strummed over her ear again.

Charlie put her book down before swirling the orange slice in her sangria with a wooden stirrer, considering what loomed attractive behind her. She didn't even need to see him to know how tempting he would look.

Her other hand gestured for him to join her, to sit to her right so that her left side, the one closest to Juliette across the patio, would be clear. "Sort of. I'm off tonight."

The aroma of melon and sage cologne wafted through her senses while Gabriel gracefully took the chair beside her. "I see your colleague is working though." His tan hand with a gold signet ring on his pinkie caught the light and her eye as he gestured toward Rob.

Rob sat at the table closest to Juliette, watching the ocean vista and their mark.

Santiago was snuggled up to Juliette's right while Lindy admired her, whispering into her left ear. Whatever she just shared made them kiss. They had four more nights here in Ibiza before it was back to set, back to work for them all… and Juliette was determined they would enjoy their hiatus, no matter what had happened the night before.

It was a focus on a fun future that started to infect Charlie. Though she wasn't quite sure she could afford the affliction.

"You never did tell me." Gabriel raised his glass of bubbly Cava up to his beckoning lips, asking before he sipped, "What got you into this line of work? One I see you're still doing, wearing your boots even though you said you are off tonight."

His regard, noting details yet again about her, it greased the lock to the gates protecting her body. "I guess I can't stop myself," she said. "I've always done this. Always protected others."

"In the military?"

The answer? Yes, but Charlie didn't confirm it. Because that wasn't the whole truth.

That's not when this started.

"I remember when I was in high school and some boys on the bus were making fun of a girl because her mom was our local Sheriff. Really, they were doing it because she was so beautiful and trying to ignore them. Eventually though, they had her crying, cowering down in her bus seat. It pissed me off. I'd been bullied growing up too, 'til I beat the shit out of my own tormentors.

"So, I did it again that day. I stood up and hit the alpha boy in the nuts with an uppercut, making him leave the girl alone. It worked. She thanked me and was safe after that. And I've been an addict for it ever since."

That part of her past she didn't mind sharing. Her childhood was full of family, joy, love and tomboy adventures. Until it was ripped away from her, along with everything else.

"And yet the beautiful pugilist-turned-bodyguard is reading a peaceful, modern Buddhist classic." Gabriel's smile occupied his entire face, one amused eyebrow raised. He pointed to the cover of her book, *Peaceful Action, Open Heart* by Thich Nhat Hanh. "I've read it too. Several of his books actually."

"Then you should know from your reading—" She could really like this man. Any smart woman would sign up for him, any horny woman would lie down with him. "…karma's a bitch."

That tossed his neck open in laughter, wafting his enticing cologne her way. She joined him in the delight, smiling, chuckling at her own joke. When his eyes found hers again, she felt the drip—the single drop of heat from him over the ice that guarded her heart.

"You, Ms. Ravenel, are no bitch. That I can tell. I respect your profession. I'm smart enough to know you have to have a generous heart to want to do it, to sacrifice yourself for others."

Gabriel's gaze was on her now, not on the table of laughs and triple snuggles seated before them. He asked, "So why sit here tonight, alone, when you could be dining with your friends? Enjoying their laughs and charming company?"

It impressed Charlie. How he noticed her, read her. How he didn't judge the provocative threesome across from them. How he didn't raise his phone to record a celebrity sighting that would go destructively viral if he did. He was the only other guest on a weeknight at this small, luxurious hotel and he only seemed to be curious about her.

Charlie sipped her sangria before answering, "I'm protecting her so she can have some fun. She deserves it."

"Don't you too? Don't you ever have fun?"

"Work is my fun."

His chuckle was rich, sweet like amber rum. "That's nonsense, Ms. Ravenel. You're too breathtaking to only partake in fun at work."

That shocked her.

Sitting to her right, surely his eyes were taking in her profile, staring right at the dark pink gash across her cheek. His compliment of her beauty, the one with scars now, it was a surprise. She had assumed it would send men running away. It certainly caused questioning eyes, gawking stares or shocked reactions. But he didn't balk at it. It almost drew his body closer. It almost worked.

"What about you, Mr. Duran? Why are you dining alone and what do you do for fun?"

"I'm from Barcelona but I come here on holiday between my travels, for their best masseur, Marco. He works magic on my knee, one that aches after hours on planes, and from years ago when I ruined it with a football injury."

He stopped for two quiet sips of Cava. They traveled over his grinning lips. He wasn't intimidated by her or silence. She liked that.

"You answered one of my questions, Gabriel." The

bittersweet tart of sangria coated her tongue before she played back. "Are you avoiding the other two? Are they too incriminating for you to answer?"

A soft laugh from him again. It turned Charlie's gaze. The whites of his eyes and teeth sparkled against his tan skin. His heavy eyebrows were soft, directed toward her, attracted. The weight of his interest started to hitch her breath, started a stream of thaw down her body.

Charlie Girl, he looks so much like him. Like Kai would've looked years from now.

Dark, adoring eyes. Straight, ebony hair hanging long enough for a ponytail. The only difference between Kai and Gabriel? Gabriel looked ten years her senior, making him quite alluring. And his accent felt like warm oil rubbing into the tight skin of the scars down her hidden body.

"You don't let a man get away with anything, do you?" His smile tickled over her flesh, making the soft blonde hairs on her arms rise in recognition.

Yes, Charlie Girl. He wants you. So much. What do you want?

"No, I don't," she answered.

He took a cigar from his linen jacket pocket, clipped the end while he answered her. "For fun, I smoke these." He brought the cigar up to his nose for a deep inhale, smiling like he relished the quiet moment, like he relished taking his time with anything that brought him pleasure. "I travel. I sail. I read. That is my fun."

Charlie turned her gaze back to Juliette. Then to Rob who wasn't watching his mark. He was watching Charlie, a knowing smile lifting his face. She could read his amused eyes. Rob was urging her to do this. Hoping she would finally punch her ticket to the adult amusement park of sucks and fucks. That she would finally end her lonely streak and take this sexy man to bed, letting him fuck her well (oh, she knew he could), letting him cure the years of ache she felt.

She and Gabriel sat poised over the possibility as their hotel sat poised over a cliff.

And that's what it felt like to Charlie—the edge of a cliff, over a fall she did not want to take.

Not again.

"And I'm alone—" Gabriel filled the silence Charlie was willing to let linger. "…because I'm a widower too."

The reveal squeezed Charlie's bruised heart. It was too much, too close to her own pain. "How?"

"Breast cancer," he said before a first puff from his cheeks. The sweet aroma filled Charlie's nostrils along with a familiar grief, one they both shared. "Maybe one day, if I smoke enough of these, I will get to see her again."

"You don't need to smoke those. We all meet our end, some of us sooner than others."

"I'd prefer sooner rather than later." He set it down in the ashtray. "And I'd prefer the honor of your company tonight and many more until then." The desire in his eyes toward hers warmed her thighs. "All due respect to my late wife," he said. "I have to confess that you, Ms. Ravenel, are the most captivating sight I've ever set my eyes upon. I know I'm being bold, but only a fool would pass you by."

The compliment shook her head in refusal. "I'm a scarred-up, tomboy wearing tactical boots and an armor of fuck-off. Not very captivating."

"You are oh so wrong and oh so beautiful. Your long blonde hair is heavenly rope for any man's desperate grasp." His hands mimicked the passion in his words.

"You have eyes like my native ocean, eyes a man would gladly drown in, yet a smile from your lush, pink lips would gift a man with life." Lava paced words poured over his lips, trying to melt her resolve.

"The trail of little freckles sprinkled across your perfect nose, across your beautiful face? A man would follow them to his death." His smile wouldn't relent. "And despite how you try, it is in vain. You cannot hide your sexy body."

It shocked her impressed, amused. Was it a load of crap or a lot of allure? He took another sip before he grinned, shameless with his seduction. "I watched you from behind my book yesterday by the pool."

"I know. I saw you there." His observation didn't bother her. No. She felt another warm drop fall. "You were reading Isabel Allende, an impressive choice for a man."

"I'm drawn to strong women. Any real man is."

Another puff filled his handsome cheeks. Charlie let them both swim in the smoky moment, not needing words, only agreeing, only seeing a man who meant it.

After one more puff, he snuffed out the cigar. Pushing it to the side, clearing his path toward her, he leaned forward, just slightly. "I thought you were so focused upon your friend and her pursuit that you weren't aware of mine. How the sight of you gave me pleasure too. I couldn't focus on my book. All I wanted to do was unwrap you and your silky, white robe."

"Are you trying to get laid, Mr. Duran?" Her tone joked but she wasn't. She didn't believe the adoration. Not for her.

"I'm trying to give us permission to enjoy a night we both deserve and want very much." His long fingers tucked his dark hair behind his ear, clearing his eyes to smolder for hers. "We don't have to feel guilty, Ms. Ravenel. All we have to feel together is pleasure."

The bold but gentle offer lifted Charlie's cheeks up in a grin.

Oh yes, Charlie Girl. You can see it.

It was in his eyes, telling her imagination exactly how.

How her fingertips would savor his incredible, tan soccer physique. How his soft lips would thrill across the taut flesh of her nipples, his long hair traveling down between her thighs, his tongue going from tender to a torrent across her clit. How he would indulge her over and over before she took control for a sensual ride that would have them moaning all night.

Because she could tell. A man like him. Powerful. Confident. Maturity making his lavishing prowess much more tempting than a sudden, selfish younger man. Yes, he would know her needs before she moaned them. He would know every spot before she pointed, probably introducing her to even more. And he would take his exquisite time, waiting for her, his pleasure coming from hers. Again, and again.

Her mind summoned all the sensual fun they could have. It made her body budge from numb to nearing warm and wet.

But her heart wouldn't dare move. It wouldn't risk pain

again. It still wasn't healed from the last wrecking loss.

"I'm very flattered, Gabriel. And I needed to hear that, thank you. That a man as kind and sexy as you still finds me attractive, even after this." She gestured to the trauma across her cheek… and to so much more. "But I'm not ready yet."

Their shared grief didn't require for her to explain why.

"I've learned since my wife died, that sometimes, when you don't find yourself ready, you let someone slowly, and very gently, guide you there." His hand reached out for hers resting on the mosaic tile table. "Will you allow me the honor, Ms. Ravenel? Even for only a night?"

She pulled her hand away, only allowing her trigger finger to linger over his hand. "Call me, Charlie."

His palm turned up, open to hold her hand, wanting more of her hesitant touch. She hadn't held the hand of a man in so long, not one offering such allure, such adoration. He asked, "Will you allow yourself the pleasure, Charlie?"

She looked over the edge of the cliff, considering the jump.

"Will you ever let yourself love again, Charlie?" he asked next.

Those words. "Love again." With her name. They hit too hard, shoving her back from the edge into two years before… like it was that same day again.

She gently pulled her hand and heart away, pushing her chair back from the table, quiet so as not to draw attention. Or to offend him. She stood up. Her voice, soft. Her answer, firm. "I'm sorry, Gabriel, but I can't ever love again."

Her booted foot pivoted, turning away. Away from the allure of hot sex. Away from the offer of tender love.

She couldn't do this, no matter how her heart broke and her body begged. No matter the tears welling behind her lonely, determined eyes.

She had to hide. To stay alone and safe.

Because… instinct warned her.

Some other man was waiting for her to appear in his world. Wanting her. Seeking her though he didn't know yet where to look.

She didn't know when.

Or where she would be.

Or who he would be.

But she knew.

Another man threatened to pierce her again.

Thank you for reading *Protect Her*!
I am so grateful to have such badass readers.

See where Charlie's sexy adventure takes her next.
An excerpt of *Pierce Her* is included at
the end of this novelette.

Keep reading or <u>CLICK HERE</u> to buy it now.

PIERCE HER

She's the hero. He plays one. That's why falling in love could be the biggest—and best—mistake of her life…

Former Marine Charlie Ravenel devotes her life to protecting women. A job that's left its mark on her—body and soul. When she's not working, she's safe hiding in the shadows. Alone. But when a young celebrity finds herself tormented by a dangerous stalker, Charlie vows to keep her safe.

One problem. She'll just have to avoid her client's sexy co-star—the alluring one who seems so intent on breaking down Charlie's defenses…

No one really knows Daniel Pierce. They *think* they do. Millions want him. But no one knows what's beneath his heroic veneer. He doesn't let them. Until *her*.

Charlie, with her arousing smile and razor blade tongue, attracts him like no other. He'd do *anything* to ease her pain, to make her his. How can he lure her into giving him a chance?

If Charlie has any hope of overcoming the demons of her past in time to save the girl, she'll have to trust her gut… and Daniel. But what if *trust* is a luxury she just can't afford?

Pierce Her, Book One in the Come For Me series, is a steamy, hot, romantic suspense read featuring a strong, kickass heroine who just *happens* to fall for Hollywood's sexiest man alive.

Sneak peek chapters next!

PIERCE HER

Come for Me, Book One

KELLY FINLEY

ONE

Charlie

How do you mark the anniversary of the day you were shot? Three times. Six years ago.

You don't.

She got up and did the same damn thing she'd done the day before. For hours. Now that was a celebration.

Charlie Ravenel aimed the bow of her kayak dead center through the paparazzi blasts of lights off the water, her paddle lashing fast slices across the surface. Exertion. Sweat. And yes, the pain. Pure Zen in her veins. Alone again on the brackish Calibogue sound. Nirvana.

The moon lingered in the clear day sky above. A constant haunting companion. Two worlds aligned, warning her that one day hers would collide again in another bloody show.

Until then, stilling the pummel of her paddle for a moment, she closed her eyes. Coasting forward, pulling a deep breath in through her nostrils, swimming in the silence, her mind sought peace.

"Hey, blondie. We'll give you a good tow!"

The loud shout dripped obnoxious, invading her mind and the moment.

Eyelids firing open, she clocked them. Three drunk young men leaving the island marina. Her destination and home. Their boat slowed in a bobbing prowl nearing her watercraft.

"No, thank you," she said. "Y'all ain't got anything I need." Her smile? Kind. Her tone? Syrup. Her glare? Fuck off.

They didn't retreat, sloshing even closer to her. She wanted to punch their dicks for ruining her quiet day on the water. Her daily church.

The youngest guy, red plastic cup in hand, swayed port side, wearing sunburned cheeks as flaming as the blood shot through his eyes. Staring pupils. Shoulders wobbling. "Damn bitch, what happened to your face?"

The insult sang praise to her ears.

Her gaze lifted higher. Quick calculations. How she'd take down each one of them.

"Why don't you and the little shrimp in your pants jump in with me, and I'll show you what a bitch I am?" The provocation crinkled a smile and the long scar across her right cheek, wearing it like a proud badge of, "Go to hell."

The biggest guy threw his chin up. Amused. "Leave her alone, dude." Smart.

Red cup dude with the logo T-shirt that might as well read, "Not sure of my cock or my masculinity" stumbled back on his feet when the wake rolled under them.

The third guy. A brunette at the center console steering the boat leered at her, brown eyes trickling a shiver down her spine. *Yes. He's one of them.* Guilt in his eyes and a desire to do it again. To violate. To hurt. Women.

The clinch of her molars bit down in recognition. Her stare locked on him. Not frozen, it was fixated.

Memories shot through her mind. *Blood in your mouth, trailing behind you. A girl desperately grabbing your hand. A baby's soul-shredding scream.*

Their boat swayed silent. His glare aimed at her. She didn't move a muscle. No retreat or waste of another word. She had all the patience in the world to stay in this moment.

"Fuck you, bitch." The youngest wordsmith tossed his drink over the side. The evil captain punched the throttle down, churning a hefty wake behind the boat.

She smiled. "Stand in line, assholes," and tossed the invitation over her shoulder with a leisurely stroke home.

Throwing her orange kayak onto the storage rack at the marina's dock, ignoring the day-trippers and locals gathered in the afternoon partying throng of bodies, a grin accompanied her five-mile run home. The rhythmic pounding of her shoes down sandy roads under a canopy of oaks draped with Spanish moss soothed her nerves.

Bounding through the back door of her home, silence and a cold glass of water from the fridge greeted her. She checked her phone on the kitchen island. A missed call lifted the smile on her face. Nestling earbuds in, she called her back, sounding off the second she answered.

"It's a Saturday night in London for you, bitch. Shouldn't

your hot ass be on a date or getting laid?"

Charlie lived vicariously through her best friend, joking but missing her dearly. Juliette was shooting a movie in London, going to glamorous weekend parties and dinners, calling with the salacious Sunday morning details.

Meanwhile Charlie was alone and up to her eyeballs with renovations on her home in South Carolina, and perfectly content in her solitude.

This weekend ritual with her friend kept her sane and smiling. Most of the time.

"Could say the same for you, my sweet." Juliette's warm voice filled her ears and soul. "Let me guess. You're alone in your rash guard, been on the water all day, and you have a book and shots of Tito's for company tonight."

"Yep. Hot pages and a cold drink. The perfect date."

"A six-year long lonely date for you. And a lonely month for me. It's about time for both of us to get laid."

No, it wasn't. Charlie shook her head. Alone she was safe, gazing out of the windows of her home at the dunes and the steel blue ocean outside.

"For now, my love." Juliette read her silence on the other end. "Let's just get you in a bikini."

"You still coming to see me when you wrap?" Charlie needed their Miami trip like a dose of heroin. Something to replace memories with euphoria.

"Yep. I have two bikinis, and now I'm on the hunt for a scandalous one piece. I want a red, plunging something. But everything so far makes my bum look like a pancake."

Reaching for her usual afternoon snack, Charlie cut an orange into big slices. "Bitch, please, you have the cutest ass on the planet, and ten million people have posted about it."

"You're one to talk with that kickass booty of yours. Did you do it?" Juliette asked. "Did you go shopping yet?"

A sweet section of the fruit slid over her lips as she talked with her mouth full. "I bought a bikini, like I promised."

It had actually looked kind of pretty when she'd tried it on at the store last week. Until she saw her scars in the dressing room's wrap-around mirrors under the cruel fluorescent lights. Pressing her suddenly sweaty forehead to the cool mirrors, she feared, *you can't do this.*

The idea of exposing herself scared the shit out of her. She was fearless about everything… except revealing her body. The sight of it always provoked shocked stares and rude questions.

But she'd promised Juliette. She'd do anything for her. For any woman or girl. Take a bullet for one. But she didn't give a shit for the attention of men. Didn't want it anymore.

"You'll be proud." Charlie opened the French doors, stepping outside into the warm winter day. "It's a crocheted string bikini." She almost got embarrassed by the purchase. But she'd kept her word, going as sexy as she could find. "And the top lining comes out if I wanna get arrested."

"Yes, bitch. Or laid," Juliette blurted in her ears, reading Charlie's mind. "I love you! We're doing this. If not getting you properly fucked by a hot bloke, at least you'll lure one over for me."

"I have no followers, and you have forty million. I think it's your gorgeous face luring them over."

"Charlie." Juliette's tone shifted to serious. Charlie knew why. "I know you don't want to talk about it, but I know it's today. And I know what's tomorrow. Six years ago. I'm just sending you my love."

"Thank you." It was all Charlie could say, a familiar surge threatening to fall over her lashes. It wasn't the kind of anniversary you celebrate. It was the kind that dropped you to your knees.

A *ping* pierced Charlie's ears.

She walked back inside to her phone on the counter and tapped the screen. "Jeremy" glowed back at her. Shit.

"Hey chica, sorry. I gotta get this. Love you."

"Love you. Cheers." Juliette ended the call.

Charlie pressed "Accept" on her phone. "Your hair better be on fucking fire calling me on a Saturday," she half joked.

In the year since she'd last worked for him, Jeremy had stayed in touch, calling to talk about fishing and football. Really, he was keeping tabs on her. But he never called on the weekend.

"She says to the man with a bald head." Jeremy sounded amused, clicking his pen. "Did you get my package? It just arrived. Should be on your front steps. It takes bloody special delivery getting something to you since you hide from all civilization over there."

"Ah, babycakes, you shouldn't have. My birthday isn't until November." She kept goading him but caught the urgency. Opening her front door, securing the bud in her ear, she bounded down the steps to the driveway. "Happy fucking birthday to me." She snagged a box from the bottom step and took them, two at a time, running back inside.

"You're welcome," he said. "Lorraine Morris sent this to me last July. She was in Madrid, showrunner for the first season of *The Druid*. One of her cast members found it in her trailer the day they wrapped shooting."

Charlie ripped the box open. Shaking out a manilla folder, she flipped it open, finding photos. Two taken of an A-4 sized note penned on a piece of vellum paper. The handwriting read clear, but it looked like a printed font. The ink, blood red.

You. Will. Be. Mine.

"Huh. Somebody likes drama, even if they aren't original," she said, examining the image for any other information. "Unusual choice of paper. Architects or DIYers usually only use it. They put a little effort into it too. Who found it?"

"Kierra Williams. She was fifteen and it shook her up. Madrid police opened a case last summer but still have nothing. There's been a cock-up. I spoke to her mother who's been throwing fits about her daughter's safety. Her mother said Kierra won't say what, won't give specifics, but the girl is adamant this is about more than a note. Now they're beginning to shoot season two, and the studio has agreed to scale up cast security."

Oh, hell no. Charlie knew exactly where he was going with this, waiting for the big ask.

"The studio manager swears his lot was secure," Jeremy said, "but someone bloody got in and out without being seen. Or maybe they were on the inside all along. Which is worse? Some nutter sneakin' onto set or a creepy sick fuck with easy access?"

"What do you think?" she asked. "Is it a prank or legit?"

"That's why I'm ringing you, Charlie. Nobody has better instincts for this than you."

He was right. She could suss someone out in seconds. Rarely, if ever, was she wrong. She'd been right about the grip in Belfast who stalked Juliette. He was in her sights in a week, caught in two. And the young woman on the catering truck who took pictures on set and sold them? Charlie caught her red-handed.

Jeremy had recruited her to work on the mega-hit show *Fated* four years earlier. She protected Juliette until the show wrapped a year ago. And she earned a reputation. Toward the cast, she was at ease, funny. Toward a threat to them, she was ruthless. Her military experience working with women and girls in bad situations and gathering intel didn't hurt either.

Charlie looked at the pictures again, knew what she thought. What she sensed mattered more. Pictures weren't enough but she trusted her instinct.

"*You.*" An othering of the stalking subject. He craved hunting an object. "*Will.*" Not a wish. A command. Sure of his power. "*Be.*" Cruel. Arrogant. Women existed for him. "*Mine.*" He needed to possess, entitled to have everything.

You. Will. Be. Mine.

The effort was amateur. It twisted Charlie's gut. The threat to this girl was not.

"It's not a fucking prank," she said.

Besides the photos, the file held a sheet of paper. Charlie's gaze studied the client profile with a headshot of Kierra Williams. She was the perfect ingénue to cast—a stunning Irish girl with full berry lips, long copper hair, porcelain skin and lush brown lashes rimming emerald eyes. She had an old-world beauty with a seductive look of emerging womanhood, sure to attract viewers and the attention of many... particularly perverted assholes. But no matter how old she looked; Kierra was sixteen now and still a child in many ways.

Charlie swallowed hard. Jeremy knew her past, knew her weakness. She could taste the manipulation.

"Rob's your best bet for the job," she said.

She wouldn't go back. Not now. Six years of crawling her way out of pain. Her body was strong again. And her mind... she had control now. Almost. It was a peace she fucking paid for and was priceless. Especially today.

"Don't be stubborn, Ravenel. You were my ace in the hole protecting Juliette. And I need you again," he said. "I can't send Rob by himself."

The truth winced her cheek, hating he was right. Yes, this girl would be unnerved with only men on her security detail. And yes, *this* girl was hiding something.

She studied Kierra's picture again, inhaling a deep instinct to protect her—or any girl—from a man aiming to hurt her. But taking this assignment would challenge every breath of peace Charlie now drew.

Something compelled her to ask, "What's the timeline?" Then she kicked herself for opening a crack of hope for Jeremy.

He hissed a not-so-silent, "Yes," then said, "Pre-production is underway. Kierra, her mum and team arrive in Madrid in one week. Shooting wraps in July. It'll be five months, tops. Rob just arrived to sort his lodging. He can help you find something."

She said nothing out loud.

"I know it's short notice," Jeremy added. "But Lorraine says they can't rely on the locals, and Kierra's parents say she's not going back without real security." He paused.

Again, Charlie waited him out.

"Oh, and," he said, "I almost forgot to mention. Anders Nylund is cast for seasons two and three."

Forgot, hell. She shook her head. Jeremy knew she was tight with Anders and his family. They'd all grown close working on *Fated*. That was where she'd met Rob too. Having both Rob and Anders on *The Druid* gave Jeremy a strong hand to play.

Truth was, friends were her only family now. And Madrid? Returning to Spain after all this time… it made her think of her mom.

"Let me sleep on it." She finally spoke.

"All right." Jeremy sighed. "We have a couple of days. Take your time." His patience rang false with anxiety.

...

She showered after her drenching glide across the water.

With her hair still damp, she curled up in her bed alone, trying to read. No go. Thoughts of Kierra kept taunting her. *Yet another girl tormented by a man.* Finally, she slept, but with a gasp, she awoke to a scream, soaking wet in her own sweat.

Her fucking nightmares? As certain as the sunrise.

Tossing and turning for an hour until physical exhaustion forced her mind back to sleep, she woke again, this time to the soothing sound of a Tibetan chime, her phone's alarm.

She stood at the bathroom sink, blessing her face with a splash of cool water. The sun wasn't up but would appear on the horizon soon. She opened the doors to her balcony. A raw breeze frosted her naked skin. She never covered her body for meditation. Learning to sit. To wait. Any discomfort, part of her discipline. Her bare legs crossed, pressing against unforgiving wooden boards, finding their familiar pose.

A rhythmic breath released her haunted ego. Minutes she lost here to only this practice. When time returned along with her thoughts, compassion for Kierra filled her soul. And sick concern.

Torment was all she knew for the uncertain fate of the last girls she'd helped. Though she would do it all again, flipping her middle finger to her own life to protect them, it was a damning price she paid. Every morning, she prayed they were somewhere well and safe, but she would never know.

But you can protect this girl.
This time can be different.

With a resolute exhale, her eyes opened. Heading back inside, flipping over her phone on the nightstand, she chuckled. Two missed calls from Jeremy. One from Anders. One from Rob. Jeremy had enlisted them. They were doing a full court press. She didn't need to hear exactly what each would say—each with their own reasons why she should join the show.

She group-texted all three:

> Relax fuckers. I'm coming.

TWO

Daniel

Trapped. Uninspired. Overwhelmed. Daniel Pierce needed to shoot something.

"Mate, you forgot this." Lance Moore tapped Daniel on the shoulder with the smartphone he'd left on the back seat.

As they walked across the parking lot, Daniel's glance down confirmed a screen lit up with a constant barrage of messages and notifications. All wanting him.

"Cheers." He dropped it in the pocket of his canvas shotgun bag. Lance had introduced him to skeet shooting, and now he had to blow off steam every weekend, exploding his stress with every shot fired.

He and Lance had frequented this shooting club while filming the first season of *The Druid* here in Spain. Now they were reunited again for season two. Daniel's celebrity status was A-list. He couldn't trust many people, but Lance was discrete, loyal. He was the lead horsemaster for the show and one of a few who asked nothing of him.

Most others sharked around Daniel, hungry for a bite of him, or more.

A black 4x4 pulled into the parking lot, the driver leaned on his horn, parking next to Daniel's 4x4. The sudden blare made Daniel's driver, sitting inside, jump.

"Who's the wanker?" Daniel asked.

"It's Anders." Lance threw his arm up in a wave. "I told him about this yesterday. He asked if he could come."

Daniel watched, amused by Anders' dramatic leap out of the car, roaring a loud "Argh!" to greet them. Wanker? No. Anders was a riot. Daniel had already enjoyed several doses of his new co-star's antics that past week in table reads.

The passenger's side door of Anders' 4x4 opened. A smaller person, wearing a straw cowboy hat, hopped down from behind the door, black cowboy boots hitting the pavement.

Too small to belong to a man.

"Lance! Daniel! My men!" Wearing a mischievous smile, Anders boomed, a rifle case resting on his brawny shoulder.

"About fucking time," Lance called back. "We've got a rugby match to watch today too, mate."

"Don't I fuckin' know it." Anders laughed. "My money's on any team playing against your English Roses." His grip pulled Lance into a smack on the back.

Then Anders turned to Daniel, green eyes dancing with a devil deal. "Wanna make it a little interesting, Pierce? Put a tenner down on your boys?"

Daniel chuckled. "A fool and his money are soon parted," he said, closing the deal with a vigorous handshake.

Stroking his long, strawberry blond beard, Anders

turned to introduce his friend. "Charlie Ravenel, come meet these two tossers. One is a supergod, and the other one is a super horse's arse."

The petite figure stepped out from behind Anders.

Bloody hell, Pierce. The thought and sight slapped his mind. *Not like any Charlie you've ever met.*

Long, blonde waves fell from under the old cowboy hat. Her chin lifted, revealing arresting sea-glass speckled eyes, fringed by thick lashes under dark eyebrows. A dusting of freckles across her tan face made her look young. Wrinkles bracketing smiling eyes suggested experience. Full pink lips cocked in a defiant grin. When she turned her face to Lance first, extending her hand, Daniel stood shocked by the jagged, blush scar scraping across the side of her cheek.

Crikey Moses, Pierce and catch your breath. She's so fucking beautiful.

"Hey y'all. Nice to meet you." Her polite and professional words greeted them as she shook Lance's hand.

"I'm Lance Moore. Horsemaster on set and supergod in the flesh." Lance nodded toward him. "That's Daniel. He's the tosser."

When her eyes landed on him, lips challenging, "Oh, I can tell," a smirk crimped her cheeks… and that scar.

So much for polite, so much for professional.

They all chuckled, including Daniel, who didn't need reminding that his face was one of the most famous in the world, requiring no introduction.

Her hand reached out for his. Small, tanned, a bit weathered. Her grip, firm and strong. And the heat from her palm? It gripped his skin. Hundreds, maybe thousands of hands he had shaken. None ever grabbing him like hers now. All he could utter was, "Nice to meet you."

A lie. Nice was not firing through his nerves in that moment.

"Well, y'all ready to shoot? Or are we gonna sit here and listen to Anders's verbal diarrhea all day?" Her sweet, ladylike Southern accent delivered the smart-arse joke. Daniel's breath hitched. Not what he'd expected by the look of her.

Anders laughed. "Yes, ma'am." He tried a horrible, mocking Southern accent in reply. "Let's get to shootin'."

They all walked toward the first station. Daniel couldn't help it. The question creeped out of his mouth. "Tell me, Charlie. What's a woman risking out here with two strange men and a big, crazy Viking?" He wanted to hear more of her voice.

"Charlie worked on *Fated* with me," Anders said before she answered. "She and her team saved our fuckin' arses in Belfast. Maja, the kids, and I couldn't leave the house until they came to help. I told Lorraine I wouldn't step foot on set if Charlie wasn't on the show."

"That's bullshit," Charlie said. "But I'd do anything for Maja and the kids."

"Ah, you're with HGR Security," Lance said. "I heard you guys were being brought on this season."

"Yeah, just got here yesterday. I'm here with my partner Rob Vasquez. We get up and runnin' Monday."

New cast security for the season? The news threatened to erase Daniel's sudden pleasure in her company. A twitch took his shoulder. Annoyed. She'd be focused on her work, no doubt. Work no one had told him about. That the showrunner, Lorraine, had upped the security level on set.

"I suppose you'll be working with my team too," Daniel said, lowering his brow, masking his probe with pleasantries. He employed a strong team guarding his privacy and life. But the buzz on *The Druid* was getting intense.

More security meant more scrutiny. More surveillance of the comings and goings of everyone on set. More limitations over already restricted freedom.

That's the price he paid for the job. He was the lead, bringing a huge following to *The Druid*. It was a streaming show that had one of the largest audiences ever. His fellow cast member, Mason Hunt, had his own fan base from his child-actor days and teen films while the young and beautiful Kierra Williams was the breakout star. All three were cast for their talent and tempting image. Now with Anders Nylund joining the principal cast too, the hype would skyrocket for them all.

"Yep," she said. "We're doing audits the next couple of weeks. Rob is working with the studio manager, and I'm meeting with all the cast's personal detail."

"You'll like my team." Drawing nearer, he caught a waft of vanilla from her hair. "Glad to have you on board." His arm swept forward with a bow, intending for her to walk ahead of him. To be polite. To enjoy the show.

She grinned. "Supergods before mortals." Mimicking his gesture, she refused his control.

It amused him. Her cheeky, confident rebuke. He relented, stepping to catch up with Lance in front of him. They reached the long line of tables under the metal awning and set their rifle bags down.

"What do you know about HGR Security?" Daniel leaned toward Lance while they unpacked, forcing himself to sound casual, then feeling like a prat because it was a legitimate question. Lance wouldn't care, but Daniel felt guarded in the ask, hiding the glance to the left he cast at Charlie with Anders at the other table, loading their shotguns. He darted his eyes back down before she caught his scrutiny.

"I know they're one of the top firms." Lance slid on his protective lenses. "A lot are former military. A few get into some pretty dodgy shit with nutter fans. I heard they were brought onto *Fated* after their first season. That Juliette Jones had some sick psychos targeting her. That someone from the HGR team took down a lot of threats to her and the cast."

"Wonder why Lorraine brought them onto the show."

"Guess she wanted the best."

Every production had security on set. As part of their work, they disappeared into the landscape. At least, that was how it had always seemed to Daniel.

Not this season.

Not now.

Charlie Ravenel joining the production gamed his every nerve. Who she was intrigued him as much as why she was here. And the story behind that scar on her stunning face? Intrigued was a beige understatement for what roused his senses.

—

Charlie

Relief dropped the tension in her shoulders when she turned to unpack the rifle. She had to turn away. Away from Daniel Pierce to find her breath.

What the holy fuck was that, Charlie Girl?

Her body howled awake at his handshake. At his touch. The first time in six years it had responded so loud to any man. The sets she worked on accustomed her to being surrounded by beautiful people, men, and women. She had seen, hell fought off, how such beauty was as much a burden as a blessing for many of them. She learned to treat them like nobodies. Or anybodies. It was one of the many reasons they trusted her.

But damn. Daniel Pierce, famously the sexiest man alive, possessed so much exquisite physical DNA it required a full audit. Sure, she had seen him plastered across covers and screens. A sudden flush fired up her cheeks for the solo pleasure she gave herself at the sight his photo a few times in the past. But that was a screen, a fleeting fantasy. This was him, palpable and in person. And oh hell, where his staggering bounty of beauty stopped, his sexy charisma raced, lapping her body for the win.

Damn, Charlie Girl. She adjusted the scope on the rifle. *Slow your roll. You've got a job to do. A girl at risk.*

And she'd fucking asked for this. Asked Anders where the cast hung out. Wanting to meet each one of them. Off set. In a setting where their guard was down. In a setting where a stalker may betray himself.

She wasn't wheels down in Madrid for twenty-four hours, kissing her relaxing trip to Miami with Juliette goodbye, before she found herself jumping into the damn deep end of this job. Right into the ocean of Daniel Pierce.

And it was raging wet.

Over six feet of hulking muscles wrapped down a body that famously took discipline and sacrifice to achieve. Black hair fell in soft waves, framing aqua eyes as deep as a cenote, enticing anyone to jump in. Stubble blanketed a square jaw and deep cleft chin. Pillow lips formed a perfect soft bow, almost feminine, until they flashed a white-hot, hungry smile.

He was cast as Zeus, the god of gods who had no equal, many enemies and could bed any woman in a comic book series turned movie franchise. Two films had dominated the box office in the blockbuster series. A third was rumored. And everywhere Daniel Pierce went, he was "Zeus" to his fans. Charlie read how many followers and press also branded him—"Sex God."

Practiced inhales like she used in mediation subdued the shock of him. And his question? About what she was *risking* out here. Well, that pissed her off.

You ain't risking shit, Charlie Girl. Not with any man.

Her mission clear, she racked her rifle. *Protect the girl.*

Shifting her nose down, peering covert up through her eyebrows, she studied his heart-stopping profile while he stuffed shells into his shooting pouch. A hunch drifted through her mind.

He'd gone from *Zeus* to *The Druid*. She'd watched both this week as part of her research. On *The Druid*, he disguised some of his beauty behind the auburn wig, emerald contacts, prosthetic facial scars, and scowl for his character,

Carric Morrigan. It gave him a temporary escape from being Daniel Pierce.

Her synapses fired up without prompting. It never took long.

He's hiding something. More than his beauty. What?

The question scratched at her brain, making her dismiss the tingling between her thighs the proximity of him involuntarily caused. She'd get used to Daniel Pierce. Eventually.

She had gotten used to all the eye candy on the set of *Fated*. To her, the male actors were boys playing with swords, having no real concept of war. They did stunts. She had done real missions. They were sheltered. She had been targeted. She was never intimidated, rarely impressed.

Her thoughts and gaze wandered over his peach ass in jeans. *And never be fooled, Charlie Girl. Beautiful humans can commit ugly acts.*

Shots brought her attention back to the moment, to how Daniel shot first. She watched him hit two single clays but miss the double. Same for Lance. Anders took out both singles and one of the doubles.

She waited to shoot last. Counting her inhale, exhaling into the percussion pushing the air around her. Skeet held safe memories for her. With her dad. She'd begged him as a teen to teach her how to shoot her grandfather's rifle. Every weekend found them at the range. The sound of exploding clays didn't trigger her, though an unexpected gunshot could freeze her now. Anticipating the sound usually protected her.

But something else. Something had her breathing on

a razor's edge.

"Char, no more hiding. Time to play." Anders signaled for her to take her stance and turned, beaming at her. He'd seen her shoot before.

She didn't shoot like the men. All three of them fired with their rifle ready at the shoulder. Not her. She shot out-of-shoulder with two clays launched from opposite directions. She had to wait for the first clay to appear before she could shoulder the weapon. It was how her dad had taught her.

The painful glare of the memory made her pause. His lessons weren't easy, but they had saved her life.

A life that in that moment stepped back into the line of fire. To protect a girl? She'd do it again.

Closing her eyes, she inhaled. On the exhale, opening them, she called, "Pull."

Fire, pump, hit. Fire, pump, hit. Getting the pair. Not a flinch of recoil. Out-of-shoulder again. The second pair flew. Shoulder the weapon. Again. Fire, pump, hit. Fire, pump, hit. Clay exploded into dust everywhere.

"Bloody hell!" Lance yelled.

She turned, saw his grin. Daniel Pierce's face recorded shock and awe.

Anders looked satisfied, proclaiming, "If you think her aim is fierce, you should see what she can do with her fists."

Still, by the time they finished the sixth station, the tremor had started in Charlie's right hand. She squeezed it tight, gaze locked up on Anders. They had shot together when they worked on *Fated*. He would recognize the signal. She had to stop.

The guys finished the two final stations but still couldn't beat her high score.

"Who's buying my first Guinness?" she asked, pulling off her hat and earmuffs. "Seems I'm owed three and will need to suffer through rugby on a flatscreen to enjoy them." She shook her hair out before plopping her hat back on.

"Oi!" Daniel exclaimed. "You dare to insult the greatest sport in the world?"

His panty-wetting grin told her otherwise. Eyes sparkling curious, roaming with an intensity over her that stirred panic with pleasure. Not trying to hide it, Daniel Pierce was anything but injured by her.

Careful, Charlie Girl. With a look like that, you'll have a lot more to protect than a girl.

...

What's coming for Charlie? Is it Daniel Pierce?
Or is it more?

The story continues in PIERCE HER,
Book One in the COME FOR ME series

<u>GET IT TODAY</u>

Thank you for reading *Protect Her*, and thank you for your reviews, posts and shares! It's so appreciated.

Get more free sneak peeks, sexy bonus scenes & alerts about the next book and more! Join the adventure and my news tease at Kellyfinley.com

Follow for fun posts & stories on Instagram @KellyFinleyAuthor

Join the reading group and find fellow badass peeps: KellyFinleyBooks

Show and share some Goodreads: Kelly Finley

Before you go… please consider leaving me an honest review. I'll hug you next time for it.

ACKNOWLEDGEMENTS

I have a confession. I had this entire series written. *Then* my street team and beta readers (yes, you can join!) loved Juliette and Rob so much, they demanded I write a little story for them. These characters are so loved in my heart and are so strong in my creative mind that well, this sexy adventure came easily to me. And they (characters and readers) are such good/bad influences on me that they're tempting me to write even more about them. We shall see…

In the meantime, I'm supposed to say how much I love Charlie. I can't. I feel it's the other way around. Charlie loves me. She keeps me happy and inspired even in the most difficult of times. She wakes me up (that sweet bitch) and fills my days with laughter, tears and a desire to either fuck someone up or get fu… well… you know.

To my muse Erin, my Marine with a French manicure, you wanted a smartass heroine with heat and heart like you. Hugs and here you go.

Big thanks to my beloved alpha and beta readers: Sarah, Melissa, Angela, Ashley, Michelle, Bianca, and Victoria. Y'all gotta know how much I love ya.

Special thanks to Kat Wyeth on the other side of my

world for your proofreading patience and magic. Such gratitude for Caroline Johnson who designs my sexy covers and stunning formatting.

To my cherished husband, kids, family and folks… damn, I'm thankful for you. I'll be thanking you more in books to come because y'all know I ain't done. Sorry. Not sorry.

Above all, my humble gratitude goes to the women who have or do serve. This beloved character is informed and inspired by you. While brave women make up less than twenty percent of the military services in the U.S.A., and they courageously comprise small numbers globally, they make it to even fewer romance covers and pages celebrating them. Not anymore.

I feature more about who and what influenced this badass heroine and her adventure more on my website. Let's get to know each other at kellyfinley.com.

ABOUT THE AUTHOR

This author loves writing fiction but hates writing bios. Still, if you made it to this blurb, Kelly Finley will share...

She lives somewhere between North Carolina and South Carolina. For over twenty years, she has been teaching about badass women but rarely found them on the pages of romance novels. So, when the world stopped and her busy calendar cleared, this romantic heroine woke her up and she has rarely slept since.

Kelly has a husband and family who love her, despite her salty, smartass mouth. She has friends who put up with her, and only keep coming back for more. Though she has a painfully big heart, she has little patience... for bullshit especially. Because allergies suck, she doesn't have any pets so she compensates with enough houseplants to compete with the Amazon forest.

If it tastes like coconut, she loves it. If it smells like oranges, she smiles. If it looks like a beach, she is on it. And if you have read one of her books, she is beyond humbled. Thank you.

Made in the USA
Columbia, SC
04 November 2021